Sunny Side Up

⌘

Heather Campbell

Heather Campbell

Order this book online at www.trafford.com
or email orders@trafford.com

Most Trafford titles are also available at major online book retailers.

Printed in Victoria, BC, Canada.

ISBN: 978-1-4269-2968-7

*Our mission is to efficiently provide the world's finest, most comprehensive book publishing
service, enabling every author to experience success. To find out how to publish your
book, your way, and have it available worldwide, visit us online at www.trafford.com*

Trafford rev. 05/05/2010

 www.trafford.com

North America & international
toll-free: 1 888 232 4444 (USA & Canada)
phone: 250 383 6864 ♦ fax: 812 355 4082

DEDICATION

I dedicate this collection of stories to my family and friends — life's greatest blessings.

Contents

That's Life

1."What Goes Around, Comes Around"   9
2. Grandma's Rocking   12
3.How May I Help You?   15
4.Let Us Break Bread Together   18
5.Misfit Me   20
6.Multi-tasking Decline   23
7.Obama Daze   27
8.Stealing the Joy   31
9. The Invasion   33
10.The Scavenger Hunt   38
11.Volkswagen Vagaries   41
12. Weight Loss Conundrum   43

A Peek-at-the-Past

1.The Rocking Chair   49
2.A Brief Meeting With History   50
3.Christmas in Coe Hill   53
4.Rightfully Restored   57
5.School Tales   59
6.Take a Powder   63
7.The Church Concert   69

Murphy's Law

1.The Minister Meets the Mechanic   75
2.Bus Driving Apparel   77
3.Monetary Trouble   80
4.Shades of Houdini   82
5.Take Me Out to the Ball Game!   85
6. You Know You Are Having a Bad Day
When...   88
7.A Force Not To Be Reckoned With   90
8.Computer-Savvy   92

9.Easy Come, Easy Go 95

10. E-Z-Tag 97

Celebrations

1.You never Know What Christmas May
Bring 105

2.Bacon for the Weekend 108

3.Barely Seventy 112

4.Surprise! Surprise! 120

5.The Purr-fect Twenty-fifth 125

6.Whose Turn is it? 127

Creatures, Loved and Unloved

1.Who's the Master of the House 133

2.Bolted 134

3.Down by the Bay 136

4.Man's Best Friend 138

5.The Rescue 140

6.The Watchdog and "The Rocket" 142

Reflections

1.Tea Cozies 147

2.Sentimental Attachment 150

3. Mice Phobia 152

4.Deceleration Of Time 154

5. "Dinosaur Penmanship" 157

6.Electronic Pastimes vs. Traditional 160

7.Income Tax Madness 164

8. "Another Time, Another Place" 165

Acknowledgements

Thanks to many, many people, I have been able to write these stories over the last three years and now offer them for your enjoyment. I thank all those who allowed me to write their personal stories and gave permission for sharing them in this collection.

I especially thank Sherrill Wark of Crowe Creations for her editing and helpful suggestions. Once again I owe so much to my husband Frank for all his technical help in the final birthing stage. Both he and I are proud of the cover design choices offered to us by our granddaughter Amanda (a Print Media graduate) and for her help in acquainting us with the intricate features of our new laptop.

The cover picture we chose is one of many snapshots that I took of the cheery sunflower crop on Larry and Christine Reaburn's farm located on nearby 6th Line. Something about the uplifted faces of these flowers always brightened my day, just as I hope my stories will brighten yours.

As always, thank you to the members of the local writers' club, "The Henscratchers", for your support and to my CAA friends who exemplify the motto of "writers helping writers".

Lastly, it is because of the positive feedback I receive from you, my readers, that I continue to publish. Thank you for that encouragement.

That's Life

Son Kevin, Daughter Laurie, Husband Frank and Author in front of the lilac bush in its early years.
(Page 9)

"What Goes Around, Comes Around"

It's strange how possessive a person can become over a lilac bush. Of course, this wasn't just *any* lilac bush. Thirty four years ago, Frank and I had moved to a brand new house in the captivating Ottawa Valley town of Beachburg. Although there wasn't a barn in sight on the property, and the only vestige of farm life was the corn stubble that remained from the previous year's crop, the senior villagers referred to us as The People On The Old White Farm. In truth, we were the second house to be built in a new subdivision. The farmland had been sold to a developer and the farmer's little house had been jacked up off its foundation and moved to a new location. The red brick bungalow that we purchased was a neat- looking house, but the land on which it sat cried for trees, flowerbeds, grass, and overall landscaping. The view from our large picture window offered nothing of beauty. Especially offensive was the Hydro pole and its support cables at the corner of our yard.

When Frank suggested we bring some of the lilac bush from his boyhood farm at Lake St. Peter to plant on our new property, I knew right where I wanted it to be.

"Let's hide that ugly pole," I suggested.

Frank had fond memories of his cousin and him sleeping under the huge lilac bush on summer nights at the farm. I think he would have liked to have chosen a spot on our property that might, in some future year, have afforded this treat, but he knew the bush we were bringing would take several decades to reach the size of the lilac grove of his boyhood years, so he agreed to my choice.

Even though the bush itself grew rather quickly, putting out new offshoots each year, it was seven years before the first flowers appeared. By then, the foliage was hiding the bottom six feet of that ugly pole. To add to this beauty, the heavenly smell from those deep purple lilacs filled the air. I gathered bouquets for the house and the fragrance wafted to every room.

Year after year, the bush continued to be more bountiful. One spring day, a neighbour about twenty years younger than I, hurrying by on her morning walk, stopped when she saw me getting into my car to tell me that she had picked a bouquet of my lilacs and hoped I didn't mind. I'm not sure what kind of medication I was on (it was during those notorious menopausal years, more appropriately in this case, mental-pause) but I replied curtly, "No, but I wished you had asked me first."

She looked crushed, mumbled something apologetic, and left quickly. I stood there stunned, sure that if I'd looked in a mirror, warts would be showing and my broom would be standing behind me.

All day at work, I fretted over my mysterious performance for which there was little justification. The next morning, prepared to apologize, I walked down the street to this young woman's home with a bouquet of the lilacs. No one was at home. I left the lilacs and a note. I never did receive an acknowledgment. She probably had decided it was wise to keep her distance from such a crazy lady. She and her family moved away shortly after this incident. I sincerely hope I was not part of the reason.

Unknown to me, the lilac bush's expansion (that I felt was a blessing), was causing some concern to other residents. Our bush is on the corner of the T-intersection that our street makes with the main road. There is a stop sign, but apparently, drivers felt they had to inch out ever- so- carefully to see around our bush.

I was made aware of this when municipal workers called at my door, explained the issue, and asked if they could trim it. No hysterics from me this time. I agreed, although I did mention the sentimental attachment of its having come from Frank's boyhood farm. This visit, and the subsequent trimming was repeated every two or three years.

Last year was a different story. No one called at our door, nor was there a phone call, nor any kind of notification. I came home early one morning after having been away the day before and, to my horror, there was nothing left of our beloved lilac bush except roots and stubble! I stood in disbelief, numbed by the callous destruction.

Yes, I complained. The councillor explained that the maintenance crew was new, and ambitious, but he also pointed out that our bush was on road allowance. Getting our permission for previous trimmings had been a courtesy, not a necessity. I wondered at the time about our courtesy in mowing that same road allowance year after year.

Now it's spring again and we miss that bush. Is this my nemesis for the absurd, insane behaviour I showed to my ex-neighbour? Maybe. My consolation is that the lilac bush will grow again from the remaining stubble. On the other hand, my friendship with my ex-neighbour will likely never have such a chance.

Grandma's Rocking

Stressed-out nine to five workers often say "I'll be so glad when I can retire." I hesitate to ask them what they think that will be like. I've been retired from teaching for more than twelve years now. I left the stress behind but I still get up at seven and often am not in bed until midnight, trying to squeeze my life into those hours. Very little time is spent in my comfy rocking chair.

Right now, I am sitting in a motel room in Belleville, Ontario. It's seven-thirty in the morning and already I've had my coffee and some fruit, compliments of the hotel. Now here I am pecking away, trying to get a bit of writing in before I meet a friend for a nine o'clock breakfast.

The days leading up to coming here were akin to a marathon. Writing is a hobby that consumes me and is often the reason that the dust bunnies play and multiply with complete freedom at our house. Last week, this hobby took me to a four-day writers' conference in Ottawa. We arranged for our granddaughter to house-sit and look after our dog and cat.

The writing conference was so well organized and so packed with workshops and networking that I awoke each morning with renewed energy and collapsed each evening exhausted, glad of the luxurious accommodations.

On Sunday morning, our son picked me up from the conference and took me to his place where I helped him plant some flowers and shrubs. It was raining so that speeded our task. With the planting mission accomplished, I pointed the van toward home. For two hours, I enjoyed music from the radio, interspersed with my alternating thoughts of the inspirational aspects of the conference and the domestic duties awaiting me at home.

Arriving in our driveway, I checked my watch. I "guesstimated" that I had seven hours before I would have to be packed and ready to go with my husband on another four-day junket, the one that would bring us here to Belleville. We were combining business (his) and pleasure. But before I could pack, I'd have to unpack.

My house set-up is rather unique in that my computer and our laundry facilities are in the same room. It's so convenient. I dumped the dirty laundry both from the suitcase and the hamper, sorted it, started up the first load and then parked my butt on the office chair.

Accumulated e-mail greeted me. Several messages were related to the local fair for which I chair a couple of committees; another concerned my job as church organist; and one was about an upcoming family reunion. I typed fast and furiously, interrupted only by the need to put wet clothes into the dryer and add another load to the washer. Over my hastily prepared lunch, I checked the answering machine, and returned messages. Husband Frank was at the cottage finishing a building project because we had a family of three arriving in the afternoon and staying for a cottage holiday. I sorted through the Canada Post mail that had been left on the table, wrote some cheques, tended to the laundry, put dry clothes beside the suitcase and then headed for the cottage.

It is like Heaven there, so peaceful and quiet. It is usually my writing sanctuary, but not today. Today, it's a case of "Heaven can wait"; the beds must be changed for the expected company. Off with the old, on with the new. I stuffed the dirty bedding out of sight with the promise that I'd deal with it the next week. A check of the refrigerator proved it was a "happy fridge". Frank must have shopped.

The guests arrive, laden with more food, and volunteer to do the barbecuing. Frank and I can take a breather and enjoy some visiting.

Too soon it's time to push back from the table and head back home to finish packing.

My house-sitting granddaughter reminds me that I'd better throw in my bathing suit too. (She knows I like to swim.) We say hurried goodbyes, then I'm "on the road again", a Grandma more inclined toward rocketing than rocking. I'll enjoy it while I can.

How May I Help You?

In the past, when wanting to cancel my local paper at summer holiday time, I phoned the newspaper office and, within a minute, the deed was done. How times have changed.

This morning I called the number provided on the front of the paper for Newspaper Sales and Service. Following the directions of the automated prompts, on my keypad, I pressed "2 for Circulation".

An officious female voice answered with "Welcome. Which of these can I help you with?" Then in sing-song cadence she spoke slowly, emphasizing each syllable: "1, de-LIV-er-y prob-lem; 2, va-CA-tion hold; 3, ac-COUNT; 4, Some-thing ELSE."

I wondered whether this was a real person or a recording. I pressed number 2, convincing myself that it must be a recording. It is not normal to speak in such artificial cadences, unless you feel the recipient is incapable of normal comprehension.

Next the voice announced: "I need to know your phone number."

I rhymed it off and was surprised at how I, too, had adopted the same cadence.

Immediately the response was: "I'm sorry. I did not get that. Please say it like this, starting with the area code." Then she, in slow, singing fashion, recites a telephone number.

I reply in like fashion, but louder because I cannot understand why she didn't "get it" the first time!

"Thank you," she says. "Now I need to know your house number. Say it like this ..." and she demonstrates with a fictitious number in slow syllables

I laugh because my house number is "one". How difficult can that be? I reply "One!" loudly. There's no way I can make that word be 2-syllables. I am relieved that the voice "gets -it" this time.

Next she wants the date of stoppage.

I started to tell her in the slow, syllabic manner, "Joooo-lie..." but before I can pronounce "thirrrr-teenth", she interrupted to tell me that the latest she could stop my paper would be –JAN-u-ar-y. I thought she must mean "soonest", not "latest". The whole operation was bizarre.

Whichever it was, the voice realized without me saying a thing, that January would be unsatisfactory: "I'll refer you to an agent. Please wait."

In less than five seconds, a polite male voice that I know right away is a real person, says hello, direct from our local office. Why did this not happen in the beginning, I wonder.

I tell him the problem I've had in trying to put a Vacation Stop on my paper. We laugh together. "Pay no attention to the machine," he says.

The delivery stoppage is accomplished in less than thirty seconds! I hang up, happy, but still puzzled as to why the machine is necessary in the first place. So much for progress by automation! When I decide to start my delivery again in the fall, I'll simply phone the newspaper office number that's given in the phone book.

Let Us Break Bread Together

Eva and Everett hurried out of the post office with their long-awaited, brown paper-wrapped parcel bearing the telltale American stamps. They urged the horses to go faster, so anxious were they to open this parcel.

Eva and Everett lived in my husband's home town of Lake St. Peter, Ontario, many years ago. They acted as guides for American visitors to hunting camps and good fishing spots. Usually they received a payment for this. One American couple was so appreciative that every year, they not only paid for the service, but at Christmas time they sent Eva and Everett a gift. Sometimes it was a food delicacy, sometimes an unusual ornament, other times, a new wallet and purse, or sweaters and scarves.

Eva and Everett had a rural address and so, in anticipation, as the Christmas season neared, they made daily trips to the local Post Office. What great delight when the parcel arrived.

Heather Campbell

This year, as in other years, the trek home was quick. As soon as they were inside the house, they ripped off the brown paper to see what treasure was within.

Unfortunately, this time, their spirits were quickly dashed when the contents turned out to be two large loaves of homemade bread.

"Why would they send us bread?" Everett exclaimed in disgust. "The bread you make, Eva, is the best. We don't need someone else's."

Eva, too, was puzzled as she put the wrapping back over the bread and shoved it aside on the table.

After a few hours, the two sat down to the evening meal.

"Well, I guess if it's here, we might as well eat it," Everett announced, pulling the one loaf out of its wrapping. "Hand me the bread knife."

He placed the large knife on the middle of the loaf and attempted to cut it in half. With each sawing motion, a grating sound emitted. "What the heck is going on? Is this some joke? Give me that other loaf until I try it," Everett snarled.

This loaf proved no better. By now Eva was examining the first loaf and the cut Everett had tried to make in it. "Look, Everett. There's a bottle in this loaf. I wondered why it was so heavy."

19

Together they stripped away the bread to discover a twenty-six-ounce bottle of rum.

"Well, can you beat that?" Everett laughed, holding up the bottle.

It was obvious that the second loaf held the same. How quickly *these* spirits changed the *dashed* spirits of Eva and Everett.

"I think we can even use what's left of this bread for stuffing the turkey," Eva declared. "This wasn't such a bad gift after all."

"I'll drink to that, Eva. Sure glad we decided to sample that bread!"

Misfit Me

Today, I joined the Island of Misfits. Apparently, I am a rarity when it comes to bra sizes.

Over the years, as I have matured, both in wisdom and in bra size, I realized that I needed firmer support for parts of my sagging anatomy. Everything heads south after a certain age. Bras with bones down the sides and under the cups offer the best support. Men or women lucky enough to never have worn a bra will never understand how after a few hours these bones begin to dig as if they are trying to fuse with your skeleton. It is agonizing! I am one that likes comfort; however, going braless is reserved for my pajama-time only. Recently, in our local paper, I noticed an ad for the custom-fitting of bras. The advertisement promised no bones, no riding up of back-sections, no underwires, yet it guaranteed firm support in this new miracle-type bra. The appointment for the fitting was free. I figured I had nothing to lose.

This clinic would be held at a nearby hotel. I made my appointment with the itinerant lady clinician, noting the room number where she would meet me. No mention was made of the cost of the bra, but I was assured that there was no obligation to buy if I were not satisfied.

Upon arrival, I was instructed by Ruby, the matronly clinician, to take off my sweater and bra. Then pursing her lips, Ruby expertly encircled my exposures with her tape and did her "boob measurement". Next she turned to her wall of plastic drawers all labelled with numbers, such as 36EE, 34D, 38C, etc. From one drawer she selected a bra and slipped it on me, proceeding to pull each "boob" up and poke it through the hole in the front, much like most women do when they are nursing mothers. With that done, she pulled a flap up over each boob and fastened it near the base of the strap. That completed the formation of the cup. All the while, Ruby was explaining how this was a Health Bra and was so much kinder to my tissues than what I had been wearing. When she was finished with the lifting, inserting, and covering, she told me to bend over from the waist and bounce a bit to jiggle my *flesh* (her much more refined word for these global apertures) farther into the cups. I'm quite sure men have never experienced anything even remotely similar in testing their jock cup sizes!

I bounced, and Ruby surveyed the results. "No," she said. "That isn't the right fit."

She removed that bra and started over with another. Same routine, same result.

This time Ruby sighed as she selected from another drawer. "You must have quite a time finding a bra in a store," she commented, matter-of-factly.

I smiled, but was non-committal. I looked at the pink bra I had worn to this appointment, now lying discarded on a nearby chair. Although at times it became uncomfortable, it did the intended job. I had several more of the same brand at home.

Twice more Ruby went through this fitting routine with me. Finally, she shook her head, furrowed her brow and announced she had no "miracle" for me. I was one of the minute number that she could not accommodate.

"Sorry. Your size falls somewhere in the cracks." Then she rushed on. "But the company will have a new bra out soon.

You can book an appointment for our next clinic, probably in five or six months."

That's when I asked the price of the bra.

"It's $129.00. Plus tax," she said, nonchalantly.

I repeated the number, just in case I had misunderstood.

"That's right," Ruby said.

I wasted no time in donning my old faithful pink bra, thanking Ruby for her time, and hastily saying goodbye.

Happy to be a misfit, I hurried past other women waiting for their "miracle". I could spend that "$129 plus tax" on many other pleasures. I guess I'm not ready for the "Cadillac" of "global flesh holders".

Multi-tasking Decline

I opened the washer one late November morning to drop in the flannel sheets just stripped from our bed. To my astonishment, my husband's trousers and corduroy shirt were already in the washer. I felt them. They were wet. Obviously I had washed them. But when? How long had they been sitting there in this sodden state?

I pulled each item up to my nose, relieved when they passed the sniff test. Thank goodness it was cool weather. Taxing my 67-year-old brain, I tried to recall just when it had been that I had put these clothes in the laundry. (The trousers were newly purchased and very expensive. What if they had shrunk?)

I decided that it must have been Monday. I had been racing around to clean up the house — well, at least the bathroom, kitchen, and dining room that I thought my fellow-writers might use when they met at our house that night. I now had a faint recall of finding these items in a half-hung state on top of the clothes hamper. I had wondered at the time what had deterred my husband from opening the lid and putting them in? I must have headed them direct to the laundry. *Out of sight, out of mind.*

With that mystery solved, I grabbed my Swiffer, worked its magic on the kitchen floor, then took off the dusting pad sheet and attempted to put on a clean one. Why was it so short and not fitting the pad? Would you believe I was attempting to attach a fleecy dryer sheet instead of the dusting sheet? What is happening in my brain-cell department? I used to be the queen of multi-tasking!

Facts from articles that I had read about dementia and Alzheimer's disease flitted through my mind. Had I cooked with aluminum pots and pans too long? That used to be one theory for what might cause Alzheimer's. I'm using Teflon-lined pans now. My husband jokes that he doesn't see how that will help because now our memory just "slips away".

Last week, I turned on the tap and was running myself a bath in our whirlpool tub. It takes a while so I left the bathroom and started to do some hurried tidying. I picked up my husband's shirt and muttered to myself that it should be in the clothes hamper. I was in and out of most rooms in our house in my "picking-up frenzy". Soon, I could tell by the sound of the water that the tub was reaching the full mark. I charged back to the bathroom.

No, the tub was not overflowing but floating at the top of the water was that shirt.

Now, my husband jokingly tells people, "We are going green at our house."

Using the same water for both bathing and laundry had not been my intention. If the wet evidence had not been staring at me, I would have argued with anyone that I had put that shirt in the clothes hamper.

I squeezed out as much water as I could, added a few other items and did an unplanned laundry, but in the washing machine. While it was on spin cycle, I tried to unwind from mine. I turned on the jets, eased into the warm bath and took a few minutes of quiet meditation. It was difficult to blot out thoughts of *my condition*. When I used to be able to accomplish many tasks at once, my son labelled me as being "in overdrive". Now my label might be "not operating on all cylinders"!

In the past I had taken a dim view of the males at this house who did only one thing at a time. For them, setting the table involved trip after trip from the kitchen to the dining room. Making the tea, stirring a pot, or making the toast was never even attempted until the table-setting was finished.

Apparently, I may have to adopt this trait of "one thing at a time". It appears that I need to concentrate fully on the task at hand. Have I gained an unhealthy measure of testosterone?

To cope with my "out of sight, out of mind" malady, I now have such things as important letters, tickets to a performance, garbage schedules, etc. attached to the front of my fridge. Along with the pictures of my grandkids and the assorted magnetized mementoes displayed there, it's a wonder that the weight of it all doesn't cause the refrigerator to fall on its face. When company is expected, I whisk all that important — and sometimes personal — info off the fridge and into a plastic bin. I stick it under the bed until the guests are gone.

I'm also using acronyms to help me remember what few things I need to pick up at the store. I hate to have to rely on a list for getting three things as simple as milk, eggs, and bread. I tell myself MEB and, so far, this has worked. The day I come home with milk, eggs, and bacon, I'll have to change tactics.

When something is of utmost importance, I write a one-word clue on the palm of my hand. Perhaps I need to update to a

Blackberry?

Having recently read that drinking tea may improve and maintain brain health and function, I'm increasing my consumption. Apparently, it even helps to restore damaged cells. Pour me some more! I may have a chance to get all cylinders operating after all!

Obama Daze

I'll not forget the Tuesday, January 20, 2009 inauguration of Obama, the first black U.S. president, but not necessarily for the normal reasons.

Although I had watched the actual ceremony, when Wednesday morning's Canada AM featured the highlights, I gravitated to my rocking chair to watch once more, soaking up every detail, hanging on his every word. Periodically, I looked for my day's agenda but it was nowhere to be found. Why is it that a good share of my day is spent looking for things I have misplaced?

Two hours later, at 9:30 a.m., I had run my bath and was leisurely stepping into the tub when something twigged in my head that this was Wednesday. Now that I am retired, I go every Wednesday to Country Haven, the local seniors' residence, to help with a craft group. The group starts at 9:30. I have the key for the supply cupboard, the cupboard that should have been opened fifteen minutes ago!

Now immersed in my bath, I grabbed the phone I keep in the bathroom (people tell me this is dangerous but, so far, no accidents). I was hoping that the Activities Coordinator had opened the cupboard and enough helpers had shown up that my presence wasn't missed. Unfortunately that was not the case: the co-ordinator had opened the cupboard but Volunteer Ethel was all alone.

"I'll hurry," I said. My bath became a dip, and my choice of clothing was whatever was handiest. I made it to the group by 10:05, trying to blame it all on misplacing my agenda. (I am probably no longer on Ethel's Christmas card list.)

This was also the day that Frank and I had to go to Ottawa. Early the next day, he was to have a biopsy because he had volunteered to be part of a cancer study group. Today would be a little shopping and getting settled at the Rotel Lodge where we would spend the night.

About five miles away from home, Frank said to me, "Did we bring the papers I need for tomorrow?"

(Why is it that "we" really means "did Heather bring the papers?")

At the moment of the questioning, I was reading "Obama mania details" on the first page of the day's paper.

We headed back to our house in Beachburg. At least I can give myself credit for having the papers neatly filed and ready.

We are back on the road in record time but then Frank asks, "Did we pack my eyedrops?"

I counted to ten. I had asked just before we left if there was anything he needed from the bathroom besides his shaving kit. So we turn back again. As I hurry from the van to the house, I'm imagining that we are providing our neighbours with their laugh for the day.

Finally we actually do make it to the Bayshore Mall. I'm set to shop. Frank by now is "Homer Simpson"! Did I mention that he is on Day 4 of his no-smoking program? He says he will stay in the van and sleep while I shop. Oh, joy!

Shopping for a red mock turtleneck sweater, the only thing I really wanted, proves tiring and futile. I am *becoming* a turtle as I trudge from store to store. So far, I have purchased only a set of towels. I decide to head for the van. On the way, I pass a newsstand selling the "Souvenir Edition" of the Obama inauguration. I add it to my towels.

Next it's off to another mall to check on how well my book sales have been going. That is a little more encouraging. "Homer," who would prefer a cigarette, grudgingly goes along with my suggestion that we eat at the nearby restaurant. That is, until I decide we should phone ahead and check on our room. Using our cell phone, I attempt to call the number but a recording tells me that we have no more minutes left on our phone account. "Homer" is mad at the whole world now. So much for the happiness that normally goes with a dinner date!

Thank goodness our room was still reserved for us and we slept peacefully.

The next morning, we are up early and head for the nearby hospital. The instructions had said: "No food or drink after midnight." Frank abides by this and goes to the seventh floor. I have a leisurely breakfast in the cafeteria and am just looking forward to some reading time when Frank reappears.

"Boy that didn't take long," I remark.

"That's because it didn't happen. I had not been prescribed the correct antibiotic. Now I have to come back next month. Let's get out of here."

By this time I've started putting on my coat.

"Do you know what else?" Frank says.

"What?"

"I think we forgot my shaving kit in the hotel bathroom."

I try to ignore that all-encompassing "we".

"We" head back to Rotel. I ask at the desk and am told to talk to the cleaning staff upstairs. The result: no shaving kit.

Back in the van, I decide to check our suitcase. I unzip it and guess what's on the very top?

"Homer" and "Marge" better head for home. I think they could be dangerous.

It's time "Marge" put away her souvenir edition, controlled her Obama worship, and, above all else, finds her agenda!

Stealing the Joy

Christmas shopping, at the best of times, is not all Joy to the World. Nor is every shopper filled with goodwill to all mankind as a recent shopping trip proved. I was dutifully checking off each item on my Christmas list as I trudged my way through the busy mall and my bags were getting more cumbersome. After I had almost upset a beautiful display of crystal in a gift store, I decided I'd better take my bags to my car. But the "calendar store" beckoned as I passed. Experience has taught me how difficult it is to find calendars after Christmas that fit the wooden frame that adorns our dining room wall.

My resolve weakened and I lugged my bags into the store. The display of calendars offered hundreds of sizes, styles, and art work. Selecting, measuring, returning the non-fit to the rack, and repeating the effort consumed precious time. Finally I settled on Birds of Canada, a perfect fit with beautiful pictures. The young male cashier, thinking I was buying it for a gift, even put a gift box in the bag with the calendar. In a way, he was correct. It was a gift for me.

By the time I reached my car in the parking lot, I knew I was too tired to shop any more. I buckled myself in and drove the thirty-minute trip home. After dragging my purchases into the house, it was as I was stashing them away that I realized that the calendar bag was missing. I even double-checked in my car but nothing had been left behind in it.

Disappointed and annoyed, I phoned the calendar store and the drug store that I had visited after the calendar purchase, as well as the mall office, but it was a futile effort. No bag with a calendar had been found.

I was angry, both with myself and with "the thief". I knew I should have gone with my bags to my car before I got so burdened down that losing one was easy. On the other hand, the person picking up my lost bag should have taken it to the mall office.

Four days later, after a snowstorm that shut down almost everything in Central and Eastern Canada, I read a newspaper account of a couple who not only ended up stranded at the airport instead of enjoying a honeymoon, but who had been taken advantage of by a thief who had been able to jimmy open the lock and get into their car. All their Christmas gifts, wedding gifts, and their digital camera containing their only wedding pictures had been stolen.

That certainly made the theft of my calendar become insignificant to me. It could be replaced; perhaps it had even brought joy to someone. The "honeymoon couple" might feel the same about the gifts but the real crime was the theft of the pictures that can never be replaced. I only hoped that in a day or so the news would be that the camera had mysteriously returned. Then I might be convinced that mankind *is* wanting to put "Christ" back into Christmas.

(*Author's note: Unfortunately I did not hear such news but the "eternal optimist" in me likes to believe that it did happen.*)

The Invasion

Awakened by the noise of a helicopter, Lois tried to focus. She peered at the alarm clock and noted it was half past midnight. Her first thought was that the Trenton Air base was practising manoeuvres. By the third noisy circle overhead, Lois decided she should get up and have a look. Why was the circling being repeated and why was the copter so low? She didn't turn on any lights but watched from the bedroom window. If this was a helicopter, what were those balls of fire that kept appearing and disappearing? Maybe this was a visit from outer space. Thoughts of "the body snatchers" programs she had watched flashed into her mind. Panic began to set in.

Lois and husband, Earl, live in a cozy, modern house in a tree-filled rural area near Ormsby, Ontario. Their two boys are married and are no longer living near home. At the time of this story, they had no close neighbour. Ormsby is about five miles away from Coe Hill and is a hamlet of perhaps ten homes. The source for police attention is the town of Bancroft, a half-hour drive away.

On this particular night, Lois was alone. Earl was working on a construction job about two hours away and was staying in a trailer there. Lois had gone to bed at her usual 11:00 p.m. time and had peacefully drifted off to sleep. The alarm was set for 6 a.m. so she'd have time for breakfast before leaving for her postal job at Bancroft.

It was now past 1:00 a.m., far too late to call anyone. Lois considered going outside and having a look. She watched from the window a bit longer. The balls of fire kept dropping. She thought of the nearby pond and the fish. Was this some kind of an enemy attack and the water was being poisoned. Or the air? She'd be foolish to go outside and breathe in that poison!

Other than the balls of fire lighting up the sky on a rather regular basis, it was pitch black dark. Turning on her lights would tell the world she was there. Lois decided she didn't want "the enemy" — be they terrorists or Martians — to know her whereabouts. The circling by the aircraft with its bursts of fireballs kept repeating. Minutes became an hour, then more. Lois tried to think rationally but she was scared. Would she even be alive in the morning? When might someone find her? And in what condition?

Rural people most always have a flashlight ready. Lois used hers to help her find a pen and paper. She sat at the kitchen table and shaded the light with her hand as she hastily scribbled a note as to what was happening, a note for whoever would find her. The note read:

Dear Earl and family: An invasion of some kind is happening. I'm afraid to go outside. There are balls of fire dropping and something keeps circling overhead. I have the doors locked. I love you all.

Lois

She wondered if she should call the police. But what could they really do? She knew Earl did not have a cell phone and there was no way of being able to talk to him. Oh, how she wished he was home here with her! Finally, after much pacing, she crawled back into bed but she could not sleep.

The circling and the fireballs finally stopped as dawn appeared and she knew she had dozed off when the alarm clock's rude ringing awakened her. She still had no idea who the invaders had been, but she knew by the note on the table that she had not been dreaming. Everything outside seemed peaceful and she could see nothing out of place. Lois was glad to be alive. She'd maybe phone someone in Ormsby a little later, but right now she needed breakfast and a coffee. She was developing a headache, not unusual, considering the night she'd had. Lois was heading for the cupboard when the phone rang.

"Good Morning, I guess you've had some excitement up there." Lois was so glad to hear Earl's voice.

"Excitement?"

"Yes, I guess the army has been looking for Destiny King. You know, Ken's little girl. I think she's about two and had been visiting her aunt. She disappeared yesterday afternoon."

Lois had not turned on the news. "Oh how awful! Have they found her?"

"Not so far. It sure was cold last night. I can't imagine a little tyke like her out all night. The search is continuing this morning."

"Well, I sure hope they find her. Earl, I've had a terrible night." The tears that she had held back until now streamed down her face as she proceeded to tell about the "invasion" and the balls of fire, wondering at the same time if Destiny had been snatched, but afraid to even voice that thought.

"Those would be the flares they were dropping to help find Destiny," Earl said.

There was silence as Lois turned that over in her mind.

"Well, I didn't know that. Does that make me stupid? I was really frightened. I thought I might be part of a body snatchers plot! I'll be a zombie at work today. I think I slept maybe an hour before all this started and just dropped off again after the sun was coming up this morning. Now I am fighting a headache."

Later at work, Lois learned that Destiny had been found in good health in spite of the cold night temperatures. Her aunt's dog had followed her into the woods when Destiny had gone looking for her father. The dog had curled up against her and had kept her warm. She was found sound asleep with the dog nestled against her.

Perhaps this loyal pet was a bit wary of the flares and was glad to have Destiny's company. No matter what, he was the hero of the day. Whether Destiny was concerned about the flares remains a mystery. It would seem that in her innocence, she'd had far more sleep than Lois.

All in all, albeit for different reasons, it was a night that neither the King family nor Lois would ever forget.

The Scavenger Hunt

I really thought I was done with such hunts. Scavenger hunts are exciting when you are young. I remember as part of a youth group the fun we had with the list of things to find and the clues we needed to lead us to these things. We raced to see who could finish first. It's not what I would choose in this sixth decade of my life. Innocently enough though, today, the last Sunday of December, I became part of something similar. It all took place in one of our leading big-box stores.

Every week there's a huge bundle of flyers stuffed into our local newspaper. I sort out the various sales. Reduced prices after Christmas are very tempting.

Last night I checked the articles that interested me, all from one store, and noted that the sale started on Saturday. It was already Saturday evening.

Experience has taught me that sales are quickly sold out, so I broke my cardinal rule regarding Sunday shopping. After church, I made the fifteen-minute drive. In my purse I had the list of wanted items, along with sizes and prices. With that being my only "game clue" I thought I'd need, I naively entered the "play area" through the central double doors and passed the cashiers at their check-outs.

Armed with a cart for collecting my loot, I headed down the aisle to where I assumed I'd find the plastic storage containers I wanted. Alas, on the shelf underneath a huge empty space was a sign indicating that the containers should be there. Surely the store had more. This was only day two of the sale. Customers, now clearly my opponents, jostled me, grabbing other "good finds" all around me. I decided I'd better carry on with my list quickly.

I snatched the last pair of lined work gloves from a nearby shelf, smiling about my good fortune. Then began my search for the Pyrex bowls — the perfect item to put with a cookbook for a shower gift. Having no luck in finding these, I raced to find the pumice hand cleaner. A tired clerk told me the hand cleaner would be on the far side of the store, then she left me to my own devices. By then I'd pushed that cart up and down so many aisles, I was wishing I had wheels on my shoes. I made one more futile try to find the bowls. I still had ten more items on my list. It was then I noticed a clerk helping an older woman at a computer by which one can learn if the store has the item in stock. Perhaps she could help me, too. In fact, at that point, I was thinking that the idea of staying home and shopping on-line had merit. I'd truly save energy.

This very amiable, young clerk checked everything on my list, saying "I might as well learn where these things are too."

I surmised that she must be fairly new on the job. Having written down the locations, she came with me to track down these articles. Now we were a team, geared to win for sure! The trouble was that the location of many items (such as dish detergent) was listed simply as "bin". A supervisor explained that those things would be in displays in the middle of the aisles. Well, that was correct. There seemed to be no rhyme or reason to the way these objects were exhibited, but by persevering, and having no qualms about circling the area many times, we eventually found the wanted items and checked them off my list.

Did I find the Pyrex bowls? Yes. The signage had fallen down so this made the hunt more challenging but they were in a "bin".

My last mission was to head for the other side of the store to track down that hand cleaner. As I helped myself to the last two bottles, I wondered what the people coming to this sale tomorrow would find. Would there be restocking? Or would customers be told — as I was when I looked for garbage bags — "Sorry. We're all sold out."? But, should a true scavenger give any thought for others?

My check-out receipt told me I had saved $46.10. Penny
-wise I had. Energy-wise, I was exhausted! I definitely had not
had fun. I think, from now on, I'll just put those sale flyers into
the recycle bin. That will be a double energy saver. Like I said,
I'm too old for scavenger hunts!

Volkswagen Vagaries

Husband Frank has fond memories of escapades that
took place after the regular workday when he was young and
employed by the Department of Highways.

One summer, his crew was stationed at Combermere,
Ontario. The days were long. Most of the men did not go home
at night, trailers provided adequate but not fancy living quarters.
A game of poker and a few "pints" was often the pastime in the
evenings. Sometimes, friends from other locations joined them.

Such was the case one night when Murray and his designated driver, Dave (probably best not to divulge last names),
arrived in Dave's Volkswagen. Murray was keen on being part
of the game. Dave was content to watch.

Gambling has a way of capturing you. It was getting
later and later. Dave was concerned about work the next day and

suggested two or three times that he and Murray go home. But always, another hand was dealt, and the game continued.

Finally, Dave had had enough. "Murray, I'm going to the washroom and then I'm going home. You can come or you can stay."

I'm not sure whether Murray was on a winning streak or whether it was a case of trying to win back what he'd lost, but he was definitely not ready to go home. He had once owned a Volkswagen and knew that the bucket seats were fastened in by only two little screws.

When Dave returned from the washroom to his car, much to his surprise, there were no front seats. An upside down wooden Coke box sat where his driver's seat had been. He walked around the vehicle, hoping the seats were sitting nearby but there was no sign of them. It was dark and impossible to see into the woods nearby. If he had, he would have seen the two bucket seats behind some bushes.

Dave knew he'd been outwitted and outnumbered. He had only two choices: sit on the Coke box and drive home and maybe never see the seats again, or wait for the game to be over. Dave had often heard the expression "He had him over a barrel," but now, here he was, over a Coke box.

I think the first qualification for working for the DHO should have been: Must have a sense of humour.

Heather Campbell

Weight Loss Conundrum

The fun of shopping for clothes had just taken a U-Turn. The sales clerk had politely suggested that I might want to look at clothes on the other side of the store. That's where the size 14W to 22W (or more) are — the W standing for weighty women. (The sales people term it more delicately.) It was time I faced the ugly fact: I had become full-figured in every area. I spent my time looking for clothes loose enough to hide my body bulges. The salesclerk's remark was the kick-start for a diet adventure.

The very next week, I enrolled in a weight-loss program that at first caused me to be sceptical of the whole thing.

The initial fee for this program — which covers the entire year of weigh-ins and measurements — is $710.20, plus another fee of almost $400 for a green canvas tote bag filled with a starter kit of the needed essentials such as a scale for weighing food and a well-organized day-planner to help choose meal ingredients and record intake. If anything should motivate me to follow the program, that fee should. I'd be too embarrassed to admit to friends that I had paid so much and not reached my weight loss goal.

But that was not the final cost. By the end of two weeks, my bottle of capsules that increased my metabolism and my satiety at each meal, was empty. I wrote a cheque for another $42.76. These capsules contain all-natural ingredients such as pulp from the prickly pear cactus.

Why didn't I just make myself stop eating so much, especially so many wrong foods? It's simple: I don't have the self-discipline. I need a warden to check up on me each week, to weigh me, and scold me if needed.

I am also retired. Retirement and dining out go hand in hand. Restaurant meals are deadly because of the high salt, fat, and sugar content. I wanted to continue to be part of these social gatherings, so … You guessed it. I purchased a special bottle of capsules to counteract the fat and sugar so I could enjoy eating out and still lose weight!

When I complained to my coach/consultant about the cost, she reminded me that it would be worth it, and if I could maintain my goal weight within a five-pound range, my next year would be free.

To be fair to this company, I admit that their weight management program is not all about "magic pills". I am now eating a healthy diet of more fruits and vegetables, and limiting my intake of starches, fats, and salt. Colon-cleanse capsules and energy pills are contained in the fee. I am more active, and my clothes are fitting better because of the approximately two pounds I lose each week.

I am forcing myself to drink the required sixty-four ounces of water each day. The "end result" is that I can see through my pee! I hope my doctor will be suitably impressed.

According to Dr. Oz of TV fame, if a person is drinking a healthy amount of water each day, he/she will be able to "read through their pee". The male is better positioned than I for this task. So far, any reading material in my bathroom is beside the toilet bowl, not at its bottom.

In about ten weeks, believe it or not, I reached my goal. The task of recording everything I ate had been onerous but certainly helped to keep me on track. I sinned occasionally, recording a small piece of apple pie as an apple, a hot dog as bread and pork. My daughter scolded me, accusing me of "cooking the books".

About six months after starting this diet, I graduated to being on the "maintenance" phase. I feel good. I proudly wear my smaller clothes. I practise healthy eating. I try to drink the required water. I'm free of capsules. WOW! If I keep this up, my next year as part of this programme is FREE! I am glad to continue weighing in weekly, appreciating the occasional scolding, the large doses of encouragement and the motivation this gives me. I still try to keep a journal of what I eat.

Because my spouse eats at the same table, he too has reduced his weight. He has lost one waist size and I have lost two sizes.

I expect that I might be on this diet adventure for life. That's okay. Shopping is fun again. I can read through my pee. I have more energy. I no longer enjoy salty-tasting foods nor crave sweets. Yes, the trip has been costly, but it seems that even with weight-loss programs, you get what you pay for.

Author's note: I did get my second year free and I am now "a graduate" of the program. I still "eat healthy" and continue to work at maintaining the goal weight I achieved. "The warden" is not far away if I need her help again!

A Peek-at-the-Past

Betty & Wayne Heubner at the Berlin Wall on our 2008 trip.
(Page 50)

The Rocking Chair

You might wonder how a rocking chair could scar you for life. If you are three years old and you kneel in your little rocking chair, facing backwards and set yourself a' rockin', over goes the chair onto the hardwood floor. My chin must have been the first part of me to hit the floor. Sixty-five years later, I am still carrying the scar. I suppose it gives character to the underside of my otherwise dull chin.

I also still have the chair, and that I treasure. It was a gift from my Grandpa and Grandma Soble, probably for my third birthday. Maybe that is what instilled in me the love of rocking chairs to the extent that we have two in the living room, three in the rec room and two at the cottage.

The little brown chair given to me by my grandparents is quite weather-checked, having endured times outside when I would insist I had to rock my doll outside, as well as many years in a hot, dusty attic. From my teen time to my daughter's toddler time, the chair was tucked away. Then mom was glad to have it start a new life at my house. My daughter and her two daughters have all enjoyed it. Now it sits unused in the corner of our basement. I am thinking of writing a note of its history on its underside. Hopefully, one of my granddaughters (now young ladies) will want to have it as her own and someday pass it on to the fourth generation. If they do, maybe a seatbelt would be advised for those tempted to rock

like great-grandma!

Author Heather about three years of age in her rocking chair, outdoors.

A Brief Meeting with History

I'll never forget standing beside a piece of the Berlin Wall. What an impressive experience! Frank and I, in 2008, were with a tour group on a twenty-day European whirlwind trip dubbed "Road to Our Roots". As well as seeing historic sites in Poland and Germany and the cities of Amsterdam and Prague, each traveller had an opportunity to explore the birthplace or burial place of German and Polish ancestors. I was anxious to learn more about Grandpa Soble's Polish origin. Never having been an avid history buff, I can honestly say that a metamorphosis took place as the past took on reality for me.

This piece of the ugly concrete wall that we viewed, touched, and photographed is one of two or three pieces still standing, albeit graffiti-covered, left there as a harsh reminder of life from August 1961 to November 8, 1989. Before visiting this site, we had toured many cities and towns where darkened building walls and bullet holes are telltale evidence of the ruins left by war. Rebuilding and recreating is still taking place after some sixty years.

After the Second World War ended in 1945, the French, the British, the Soviets and the North Americans had joint control over the vanquished Germans. The Soviet-controlled part became East Germany. Berlin, the pre-war capital, was split into four sectors. The Soviets called theirs East Berlin. In 1961, after it had become obvious that too many East Berliners were leaving for jobs in the West, the Soviets built a wall around their sector. They had hoped to surround West Berlin and also to have it become part of East Germany. Frank's cousin, Boyd Card, was one of several American pilots who helped with the heroic airlift of supplies that allowed West Berlin to stay free of Soviet control.

At first, the Berlin Wall was only barbed wire, but in

time, a twelve-foot concrete wall was built which indeed closed the border between East and West Berlin. East German citizens were not allowed to leave the country without permission. Citizens tried ingenious methods to be smuggled across or to make a run for it and some succeeded, but it was very risky. There were nearly thirty thousand border guards. Soldiers were instructed to shoot on sight, and vicious guard dogs were trained to attack and kill.

We also visited the nearby Checkpoint Charlie museum, which has pictures and artifacts from this the most famous guard-post in the world, lasting for the entire time that the wall divided East and West Berlin (1961 to 1989). It was named Charlie simply because it was the third guard-post, the first two being named Alpha and Bravo, based on the phonetic alphabet.

Although we visited many other significant attractions, exploring the Berlin Wall area is something I will never forget. Many times since, I have tried to imagine what it must have been like to be cut off from your grandparents or from your brothers' families, or even your best friend. This happened to so many. Some have finally been able to write about it in books that I now read with great interest.

For twenty-eight years, they had little or no communication with loved ones on the other side. Those on the eastern side had a life of few opportunities, a meagre existence dominated by communistic teachings. When, on November 9, 1989, the "Wall came down", as they say, it was a jubilant time. Easterners, in joy and disbelief, streamed through the checkpoints on this day which marked the end of the stranglehold of communism. For some, it was a bittersweet day because too many years had passed and their loved ones "on the other side" had died.

My experience at the Berlin Wall was just one of many during my trip that reinforced what I already knew: I am so fortunate to have lived my life in Canada. I owe a great debt to those who fought for that freedom.

Christmas in Coe Hill

There's nothing that can equal Christmas in a small town. My childhood memories are of Christmas in the Ontario hamlet of Coe Hill (township of Wollaston, County of Hastings).

Who of us who grew up there (or in a similar small town) can forget those school concerts! I think we spent weeks practising for them. My memory takes me to the two-room school with wooden desks in straight rows, most of them with inkwell holes in the upper-right corner. Every afternoon, as the concert date drew nearer, we would push the desks to the walls so we would have floor space comparable to a stage. Then we'd practise whatever plays, recitations, monologues, musical drills, Christmas songs, or acrostics we could cram into that afternoon. Teachers of my time were: Mrs. Shirley Turner, Miss Narduzzi, Ralph MacDonald, Glen Gemmel, Mr. Johnson, and Ken Foreacre. I'm sure that each in turn wondered how they could cover the curriculum and at the same time "whip us into shape" so the concert would be a success.

The week of the concert saw the whole school body trudging from the school at one end of the village to the town hall at the other for our dress rehearsal. Both school and church concerts were held in this hall that had the perfect stage for such events.

Many rehearsals seemed to be near disasters with supposedly memorized lines forgotten and cues missed. Miraculously, each concert turned out to be an amazing success. Parents and relatives were justifiably proud of their offspring. Each year the ending was the same: Santa arrived with a gift for each participant and each teacher, and bags of candy for everyone.

Of course, both the Gospel Tabernacle and the United Church had concerts too. The bags from the church concert always had several pieces of homemade candy that the women of the church had made and wrapped the day before. Now I know how spoiled we really were!

Leading up to Christmas, the Simpsons and the Eaton's

catalogues were the most popular books in the house. Parcels were constantly arriving at the post office. Dad usually brought them home and Mom whisked them up the stairs to a bedroom. There they were opened furtively, the contents wrapped and put under the tree or tucked into a closet awaiting Santa. There was always at least one doll or game that I had wanted and lots of practical gifts of clothing or skates.

Mom loved to decorate the house with garlands and unique red and green decorations that she had crocheted. Cards were addressed and sent to relatives and friends who lived out of town. Mom kept an address book for just this purpose. I loved looking at the cards and letters that came to us. Often, Mom strung them together and they joined the wall decorations. It seemed a disappointment after Christmas when the mail became sparse. Mom would lament the nakedness of the house, too, when the decorations had to come down. She often said "It feels like someone died."

I don't think we'd even heard of artificial trees. Dad went to the bush and cut us a tree each year. Sometimes, my brother and I went with him. I remember that often the bottom two feet or so had to be cut off so the tree would fit into our living room. What looked good in the bush turned out to usually have a flat side when we got it home. That side was turned to the wall and no one was the wiser. By the time the treasured ornaments hung from each branch and the tinsel icicles dripped from any available branch space, it was deemed perfect.

What a wonder it was when we finally had electricity in our house in the 1950s. That meant we could have lights on the tree. My favourites were the "bubble lights". They had round multi-coloured pot-like bottoms and glass candle-like stems and in those stems was a liquid that bubbled inside the glass when it became warm. I doubt they would pass today's "green" concerns but no one worried about such matters then.

Some folks still remember the wonderful display of Christmas tree lights in the window of Vic and Edna Hughson's house. Having once been a commercial outlet, their front room with its large windows butted the sidewalk, and the Christmas lights provided a happy glow for people passing by.

For many years, along with Aunt Madge, Aunt Mary, Uncle Neil, and their children, we went to Grandpa and Grandma Gunter's farm house on the hill, about three miles from us, for our Christmas meal. The turkey was cooked in the oven of the kitchen's woodstove; the homemade buns with sticky sugar on the top were brought from the pantry and the crowning touch was Grandma's Christmas pudding with the thick white sauce that was her specialty. In later years we would alternate having this meal at Aunt Mary and Uncle Neil's house or at Mom and Dad's.

Dad always made sure that we had plenty of mixed nuts, hard candies, gumdrops, and maraschino-cherry-filled chocolates. Mom claimed that he went overboard and bought more than we needed, but that never discouraged him. The wooden nut bowl with its nutcrackers and steel picks came down from the cupboard's top shelf only at Christmas. It was such fun to crack open the hard shells of walnuts, pecans, almonds, or hazel nuts, and then use the steel pick to help dislodge the bits of nut within.

I never remember hearing about any debt amassing. I expect that Mom and Dad made sacrifices and tucked money away all year so Christmas could be the treat that it always was. It was a happy time, far simpler than today's celebrations. I treasure those memories.

Rightfully Restored

Friend Marilyn Coughlin tells with wonder about digging an unrecognizable old harvest table out of an ancient barn that was on property she and her husband had bought. It was filthy, covered with layers of bird poop, bits of manure, and unnamed dirt, most of it disguised by a cover of dust.

Her husband asked, "What are you going to do with that ugly thing?"

Marilyn had a plan.

Layer by layer, she scraped off the filth, unearthing the potential beneath. But even that potential was clothed in several layers of chipped paint. After several weeks, and hours of tedious labour, she succeeded in stripping off this paint, sometimes, one layer at a time. As the paint was removed, the exquisite grain of the wood was revealed. Its rebirth had made all that toil worthwhile. Now, all it required was a sanding and refinishing with a protective wood finish.

Marilyn was sure this table had been handmade and in this farm family's house forever. *If only it could talk,* she thought. *What stories it would have to tell.* There would have been birds plucked on it, roasts carved, babies born, dresses cut and sewn, bounteous meals served, and probably sums learned and homework done by the light of a coal-oil lamp perched in its centre. It would have known not only the welcoming aroma of homemade bread and pies, roast beef, pickling spices, and bouquets of lilacs, but also the disdainful smells from cleaning partridges, early home perms, and the diapering of infants.

It was a proud moment when Marilyn moved her finished work from the garage where she had toiled over it, to the house. As she stood back to admire it she said it was as though the table breathed a deep sigh and said "*Aah.* At last I'm home where I belong!"

That table became the focal point of Marilyn's farm

kitchen. Over the years since its move, it has, indeed, been gathering new stories. Three sons, marriages, babies, surgeries, baking, holidays, celebrations, and the occasional sorrow, have all been acknowledged in some way around this table. The stories, both then and now, are begging to be written.

School Tales

I am told that Eric Stevenson's father, James A. Stevenson, was a real gentleman, a soft-spoken man with not a hint of wildness or naughtiness. Apparently this had not always been the case.

Like most country children in 1905, Jimmie (as most people called him) went to a one-room school. It was in fact S.S. #6, the little schoolhouse on Powers Road, on the outskirts of Beachburg, Ontario, that is now a comfortable home owned by David and Jean Robinson.

Recess and noon hours were times of freedom. In those days there was no need of the teacher being on "yard duty" — the older children took care of the younger ones and things usually went along quite smoothly. It truly was a big happy family because so many of the children were cousins.

Across from the school were acres of farm land. The boys liked to cross the road during the noon hour and explore a bit. (None of us today can even imagine such freedom — no fear of kidnapping or attacks.) Some of this land had been planted in peas that had been harvested the previous fall and stored in a small field granary. By early spring, the peas resembled small white ball bearings. These were then sold by the landowner. Perhaps for his own use, he had left several shovelfuls of the peas in one of the bins in the granary. One of Jim's friends, Bob Wulff, was noted for mischievousness. After discovering the leftover dried peas in the granary, he and Jimmie hatched the idea that they would fill their pockets with them and take them back to school. On the way, they shared these peas with some of the other boys, too.

The custom after lunch hour was to have hymn singing and a prayer. The boys had devised a plan.

The hymn singing began and, as was expected, someone asked for the popular hymn "There Shall Be Showers of Blessings". The verse was sung without much enthusiasm but when the chorus started with its "Showers of blessings, showers of blessings we see", on the word "see", all the boys let loose with their handfuls of peas, up into the air not once but two or three times. There were great shrieks from the rest of the students and then they all turned their gaze on their teacher, Miss Sinclair. Her brow furrowed and her demeanour became sterner than they had ever seen.

"Stop that this minute!" she bellowed as she started making her way from her desk to the boys' seats — at least that was her plan.

Picture the hardwood floor, by now all covered with dry peas. Have you ever tried to navigate in a hurry on something akin to rolling marbles? To say her manoeuvres were less than graceful would be an understatement. Naturally, this added to her loss of control and to her level of frustration and anger. In her eyes, Jimmie and Bob had masterminded an unpardonable prank. This had to be reported to the school board.

The board supported Miss Sinclair in her meting out a one-week suspension to the ringleaders, Jimmie and Bob. This was an historical reckoning. No one in those days at S.S. #6 had ever received such a "justice". I guess that's why this tale has been told over and over.

***

Another school tale that takes us to a totally different part of Ontario, happened at Lake St. Peter School that my husband Frank attended in McClure Township. A certain senior lad, Peter Johnson (not the real name), not academically inclined, was noted for giving more attention to pranks than to his studies. In fact, many in that school population had gained the name of being hard to handle and several teachers over the years had given up and departed.

That is, until Mr. McFarlane arrived.

He was young, tall, and a good teacher with a no-nonsense approach. He had a heavy hand of discipline, quite literally. And so it was on a Monday that he grabbed the prankster Peter and shook him so forcefully that most of the buttons on his shirt popped off.

Peter went home that night. The next morning he appeared at school and told Mr. McFarlane that his mother was coming to see him at noon hour. Frank and his cousin, Dale, still in the primary grades, looked knowingly at one another. This was definitely a day to volunteer to carry in the wood and water at noon hour.

Sure enough, about the middle of the noon hour, they saw Peter's mother approaching. Showdown time! Frank and Dale busied themselves with an armload of wood to pile indoors near the stove — within earshot of Mr. McFarlane's desk. *Boy, was he going to catch it*, they thought.

Mrs. Johnson walked decisively up to the desk.

"Are you the teacher that shook the buttons off my son's shirt?"

Yes, ma'am, I am," Mr. McFarlane replied.

Frank and Dale stood motionless by their woodpile, waiting for the action.

"Well, I'm here to tell you," she declared, "that if you

can teach him anything, I can sew those buttons on faster than you can shake them off!"

Mr. McFarlane was perhaps surprised but not as disappointed as Frank and Dale were.

Mrs. Johnson turned on her heel and left as quickly as she had come.

What a let down! Frank and Dale, with ringside seats, and the main attraction over!

"Take a Powder"

"Take a powder", rather than being the insult it is today, was wise advice for almost any ailment in the Coe Hill, Ontario area from the early 1900s to the 1970s. The hamlet of Coe Hill is in Wollaston Township, twenty miles south of Bancroft, Hastings County. Anyone who lived from Palmer Rapids in Renfrew County all the way south to Ameliasburg in Prince Edward County would have known about the healing powers of the homeopathic powders dispensed by the Hardinge family of Coe Hill. People travelled long distances to obtain these remedies.

On a personal note, having grown up in Coe Hill from 1940 to 1960, I had several occasions to visit Mattie Hardinge. Her house was at the west end of the village and had no sign to indicate she lived there nor was there any office or examining room.

You did not make an appointment to see Mattie. It was a case of going there and taking your chances as to how many others might be ahead of you. I can remember sitting in Mattie's front room (probably about 1950), and telling her my symptoms, mine usually being bronchial related.

She always seemed quite stern, would listen intently, then pull one or two glass vials from the box beside her. I believe that box had really been designed as a large jewellery box. It had a hinged lid and individual trays, and Mattie had each section labelled with cardboard dividers

She would uncork the selected bottles, tap a little of the ingredients from each onto six or seven small onion-skin papers, expertly crease these papers down the middle, fold each end in, then interlock them. On a white envelope cut down from a regular business-size envelope, she would write something like: "Take one powder at bedtime for the next 6 or 7 days" then quickly place each of the minuscule powder bundles inside the envelope.

We would thank her, give her twenty-five cents — fifty cents sometimes — and leave, confident that we would be well in a few days. The powders always tasted good because one of the ingredients was powdered sugar.

Those much older than I would remember Mattie's father, Dr. John R. Hardinge, a licensed doctor from Britain who sailed to New York City and headed north to Canada, settling on a farm in Salem, near Coe Hill, in 1867. He did not consider moving to a different country a reason to requalify himself in the medical world. So it was, that he — commonly known as Doc Hardinge — practised homeopathic medicine without a Canadian licence and through him, two of his six children, Mattie and Nell, learned the practice. Mattie, born in 1890, never married, but devoted herself to helping others, never advertising, never charging much, and never being officially licensed. Together Doc Hardinge and Mattie practised for more than sixty years in Coe Hill.

In 1910, Dr. Hardinge built the first telephone system in Wollaston Township, one that, ironically, my parents, Howard and Hazel Gunter, eventually owned. Dr. Hardinge started this communication system — depending on Mattie to operate it and Nell to be linesman — in order to check on his patients. If you search the roadside near their old homestead at Salem, you might still find rusty lines and glass transformers, mute testaments to this pioneer system.

There must have been some years in which Doc Hardinge depended on others as operators because in 1912 Mattie moved to Toronto to live with her Aunt Emma Roblin and to work as a telephone operator at Eaton's. In 1914, Mattie was enrolled in a correspondence course offered by the Chautauqua School of Nursing in New York State, but before she could earn her diploma, news arrived in 1916 that her mother, Ida May, had died at the age of 55 years. (There obviously were some ailments that Doc Hardinge could not remedy.) Mattie, of course, went home for the funeral and never resumed her formal studies, but she did apprentice under her father, taking up permanent residence in Coe Hill by 1921.

Dr. Hardinge was a true pioneer doctor. In his obituary of 1938 we find this tribute:

As a physician, Dr. Hardinge was tireless in his efforts to alleviate human suffering. Many times he traveled miles through the woods on foot, often spending the whole night on the trail, and carrying with him, not only his remedies, but supplies of food as well. He served humanity faithfully and humbly and it might be truly said of him as it was said of his Master that "he went about doing good." (Belleville Intelligencer, Sept. 21, 1938)

Some Coe Hill townsfolk say that his wife, Ida May Roblin, deserved a special medal because of the time she spent alone on the farm raising the children in less-than-ideal conditions and with limited finances.

Both John and Ida are buried in the Salem Pioneer Cemetery, as are many of my Gunter relatives.

Yes, there were situations in which old Doc Hardinge knew that the case was untreatable. Apparently, at such times, Doc became "unavailable": He had a farm that would profit more from his attention and would be very busy there. He was needed as a magistrate. (His daughters were more straightforward toward families of terminal patients.)

In later years, with Doc Hardinge dead and Mattie doing less and less dispensing of remedies (she didn't doctor much after 1969 because she had become forgetful and difficult in temperament), her sister, Nell (Hardinge) Clarke, was called on to help. Nell, having married George Clarke and raising a family, did not practise as much as Mattie had until her later years.

Whether it was about curing an animal or curing a human, stories abounded.

My Aunt Madge King, ninety-two years old in 2009, tells of the local veterinarian giving her and her husband, Hubert, the diagnosis that their sick cows would all die. Aunt Madge consulted Nell who dispensed her "remediating powders". At regular intervals, Aunt Madge put the powders on a piece of bread so the cows could swallow this medication. All the cows except one survived.

Friends tell about resident, Lee Gordon, whose arthritis was so bad that the doctors had given up on relieving the pain. Through Hardinge's homeopathic powders, he found relief.

Research reveals that both Doc and Mattie were fined more than once for practising illegally. Although the Hardinges never asked for it, their fines were paid by their loyal patients who would have done almost anything to keep them dispensing their powders.

According to Douglas Smith's research, the most common source for the Hardinges to get their supplies by post was from the D.L. Thompson drugstore on Toronto's Yonge Street. This company still operates today, both as a drugstore and also mailing to customers who order on-line or by telephone. Even though homeopathic medicine is available at drug stores and health food shops, to me, these remedies will never equal the power of the Hardinges' powders.

Mattie died in 1976 and her nephew Oscar Hardinge and his wife, Verna, inherited Mattie's 1912 house as well as the books and literature explaining the remedies. Oscar has since died and Verna lives there only part time. If someone of Mattie's learned homeopathic wisdom occupied that house today, I would

Mattie Hardinge's house as it looks today

certainly be a patient because there was something reassuring about that short consultation period and the immediate making-up of the remedy — not to mention that high rate of cures. Yes, I would once again be glad to "take a powder".

(Author's note: Factual information was gleaned from the book The Powders of Mattie Hardinge by Douglas W. Smith)

The Church Concert

My granddaughters refer to my childhood as the "olden days". They are right, but I treasure the good memories of those days. Recall of the United Church Christmas concerts of the forties and fifties is rich. Each yearly concert was held in our Coe Hill town hall, the building itself now a memory.

By today's standards, the hall was small, but it had a large wooden stage that was about three feet higher than the audience floor level.

Coe Hill Town Hall which has since been torn down

There were stage entrances from two back corners with change rooms off each. It was the perfect place to accommodate plays and concerts. At times, portable walls were erected on the stage to give the appearance of a living room or a hotel room — whatever the setting of the drama being performed demanded.

In my younger years, I was often part of a Christmas acrostic. I followed on the heels of one of my classmates, parading in from one of the change rooms, proudly carrying in front of me my cardboard letter that had been painted and decorated with tinsel. Each of us had one or two lines to say, such as "M is for the manger that cradled Baby's head" or "A is for the angels that hovered overhead". And, if we held our letters right side up, facing the audience, we spelled MERRY CHRISTMAS or WELCOME EVERYONE. If we miscued, the audience of proud parents and grandparents seemed to love us even more. As little tots, we stole the show.

When I became older, about twelve, I think, I was often the one chosen to recite a monologue. Few of the topics and none of the dialogue have been stored in my memory banks, just the recollection of being alone on the stage with a few props: a telephone or a couple of wrapped boxes. It's amazing what little stage fright you have when you're young!

It was in those same years that "the drill" was introduced to the girls' class. When I mentioned to my daughter (now in her forties), that my favourite memory of girlhood Christmas concerts was taking part in the "drill", she retorted with: "The what?"

I tried to explain it to her and as I did, I questioned why no boys had ever taken part, although I really cannot quite imagine boys of twelve or thirteen tripping across the stage in time to the music.

Our teacher was Mrs. Shirley Turner and, looking back, I realize that she was a true saint. She devoted hours of after-school practice in getting us ready for these annual drills. I can still see her book of printed routines on which each of us taking part was represented by an x. Parading in time to invigorating march music, two lines of girls would come from opposite corners of the stage, meet each other, intersect at the correct points, parade in pairs and in threesomes, then back to single file again. Sometimes we would mark time in pairs while others performed, and then, on cue, we would have our turn. In at least one drill I can remember, we all met in the centre with arms outstretched to form a star.

We always wore outfits that matched as much as possible and, sometimes, a band of silver tinsel encircled our heads or wrists. Usually the drill ended with the entire group in a line across the stage from where we bowed to the audience as they clapped. On cue, we paraded off.

How different musical performances are today. At a concert I attended last year, the music blared and the performers gyrated in whatever individual movements they chose. I doubt that too much time was spent practising, but the students certainly enjoyed their renditions.

Whether we are talking about the "olden days" or modern times, children, parents, and grandchildren love concerts. Some Christmas traditions never die at small- town concerts: On cue, to the singing of "Here Comes Santa Claus", that jolly old red-suited elf will appear, whether it be at a school concert or a church concert, and there will be bags of candy. But what seems to be missing most is the time needed for adult leaders and children to meet and practise. Working parents and demanding after -school activities have created a very different world. What a shame if our Christmas concerts join the "ghosts of the past".

Murphy's Law

Pet Duffy in front of the cottage shop door that has been repaired twice (Page 82)

The Minister Meets the Mechanic

For several weeks after her hip replacement, Reverend Kate was not allowed to drive her car, a white, state-of-the-art, four-door Ford. It was a happy day when she, with the help of a cane, was finally able to get into her car and enjoy being "out of her prison". It was an even greater joy when the doctor pronounced her ready for her swimming therapy.

It became routine for her to don her bathing suit at home, pull on track clothes over it, grab her cane, and drive the fifteen miles to the swimming pool at the Best Western Hotel. After her pool therapy, she simply slipped a robe over her suit and drove home.

One day after her swim, she decided she needed to stop at the drive-in window of a local bank. She pulled her car in as close as she could, did her banking, and was putting the car in gear to depart when the motor quit. No amount of coaxing would start it. A few bank patrons had lined up behind, anxious to do their banking. Opening her door as much as the space allowed, Kate told the person behind her what the problem was. I don't think the reply was "Hallelujah"!

Because she was parked so close to the wall, no one could use the bank window. In her wet state she was not anxious to expose herself and go for help, nor was there room to squeeze out on the driver's side.

What to do? Sometimes, we actually have the answer to our prayer for help close at hand. She pulled out her cell phone. This might have been a good time for a direct line to Heaven, but, not having that, she called the Ford dealer.

Explaining to the service manager her problem and the trouble she was causing, she also mentioned that it was very poor advertisement for their product, to say the least.

The fifteen minute wait before the repairman arrived seemed like forever.

A quick inspection under the hood convinced this mechanic that the problem was not there. It had to be a fuse. The fuse was located under the steering wheel in front of our very wet, scantily clad, and may I say, well-endowed minister.

Try to picture the repairman slithering in on his stomach from the passenger side and, as delicately as possible, wedging his arm and head between the wet legs of our beloved Kate while his legs and feet protruded out the passenger window. If she had been wearing her clerical collar, would that have made this scene better? Or worse? I'm sure this fellow had never had such an experience before. Or since!

One of life's greatest blessings is a sense of humour and Reverend Kate is well blessed in that department. She says she couldn't stop laughing at the time of the incident and she still shakes with laughter as she recounts this story.

Bus Driving Apparel

The above tale reminded me of another told to me by friend Susan Shields who is a former country school bus driver as well as a school secretary. Her driving in the spring and summer was blissful and without incident. By late fall, with the bus door being constantly opened and closed, the drive was often cold. By winter time, sitting behind that wheel and feeling the cold winter blast every time a pupil got on or off the bus was no fun.

The early morning run to pick up the children was the worst because even on sunny days, the morning temperatures were still chilly. For that reason, Susan wore a snowmobile suit.

Country weather and country roads can be unpredictable. In the years that Susan drove the bus, it was left up to the bus driver to decide whether or not the roads were passable. Susan lived in the village. On this particular winter morning, although there had been an overnight snowstorm, the Beachburg village roads had been cleared. After debating a bit, Susan decided to at least try her bus run. To save time that morning and get out the door sooner, she simply donned her snowmobile suit right over the top of her nightie. She would look forward to the treat of a warm shower, proper clothing, and a decent breakfast when she returned home.

She found that the back roads were a whole different story than the village. The snow plows had not been able to keep up with the storm that had dumped several inches of snow. To add to that, high winds had whipped the snow into drifts wherever there was no snowfencing or trees. Sometimes the bus, a small cube-type, was actually ploughing through these drifts. Most of the children, in spite of the weather, were watching for the bus and, with parents' help in many cases, had been able to get out from their houses to the road. But, as we all know, it doesn't matter how good a driver you might be, sometimes the vehicle can no longer cope with what nature hands out. Eventually the engine just quit. No amount of coaxing would start it. Susan and her passengers were temporarily stranded.

Susan took stock of the situation, assuring the children aboard that she would get help. There was smoke coming from the chimney of the nearby farm house, a good sign.

The farmer opened the door at Susan's first knock. She told him her dilemma, asking if she and her few passengers could use the phone.

"Sure, bring the kids in. You look cold. We have a good

fire going in the woodstove."

Susan wasted no time in getting the children to phone their parents, and she explained to them the situation. Each parent, in turn, came promptly with a tractor or skidoo. I expect the children thought this was a great adventure and were even more overjoyed that they would not be expected to go to school.

Do you want me to hitch up the horses and see if I can be of any help with the bus?" her host asked.

"First, I'll phone Beatty and see what he advises." Beatty Johnson of Cobden was the owner of the bus.

"You better take off your suit or you'll soon melt."

"I'm fine. I'll just unzip it a bit."

Well, how far can you unzip before it's clear that you are next to naked?

Beattie had told Susan he'd see how soon he could get a tow truck but not to worry about getting anyone else to help.

Neither wanting to be scandalized nor to explain to the farmer and his wife that she had not come properly dressed for visiting, Susan sat sweating in her suit. The hot coffee that she'd hated to refuse did not help her dressed-for-the-Arctic situation.

"You really should take off your suit," was suggested repeatedly as more wood was added to the fire. Each time Susan tugged her zipper down just a tiny bit farther, and said she was fine.

Finally, after almost two hours, knowing that the towing requests had been numerous that morning, Susan gave up hope of any tow truck arriving, called her brother-in-law and asked if he could rescue her on his skidoo. She was doubly relieved when he arrived. She so looked forward to cooler apparel.

As Susan says, *it was a lesson quickly learned.* This error in dress code was never repeated.

Monetary Trouble

A few years ago, my friend Murray's cousin, Sharon, and husband were living at Lars, Germany, the military base. It seemed the perfect opportunity to have Mom and Dad Gutz and Aunt Audrey and Uncle Richard from Canada come and visit. Several long distance calls were exchanged and the plans were set for a two-month visit. This visit was to include more than the visiting of relatives.

" There is so much to see here. When you are coming all that way, you should spend some time in the neighbouring countries too. I can set up an itinerary for you," Sharon had offered.

Not wanting Sharon to have the expense of booking ahead — the best way to travel — the family sent a cheque from Canada to Sharon in Germany. She would use it to get the best deals from the local travel agency.

When the cheque arrived, Sharon thought it would be best to have cash for the bookings, so she had it changed at the bank into a bundle of bills.

Now she had the problem of a large amount of cash in the house while the ticket-buying could not be done for a few days. Where to put it for safe-keeping?

What thief would ever look in the washing machine? Perfect place, she thought.

Off she went to work on the following Monday. Her children were well-trained and knew what chores were expected of them when they came home from school. Dealing with accumulated dirty laundry was one of those tasks.

Late afternoon at work that day, Sharon had a vision: The children are on their way home from school. There is dirty laundry. (This was before the age of cell phones and text-messaging.)

Her trip home that day broke all the speed limits. Secretly, she was hoping that maybe, just this once, the kids hadn't done their chores.

She knew as soon as she opened the door that this wasn't the case. She could hear the whirring sound of the washing machine; it sounded like the spin cycle. She rushed to the laundry room, glad to have arrived before everything went into the dryer. She'd heard of laundered money but now she was looking at it!

If you had visited Sharon that evening, you would have seen a unique sight: the kitchen table and the dining room table were covered in thick towels on which were neatly flattened wet bills; the heat was turned up both in the house and in Sharon's inner thermostat.

One thing for sure, the travel agent would never have to worry about "dirty money" from this family!

Shades of Houdini

Strange things can happen when one is at the cottage. Alone. That's where my husband, Frank, was one frosty Wednesday last December. It had become rather routine that after breakfast, he would go alone to our winterized cottage, about a thirty-minute drive from our Beachburg house. When I could, I went with him, but too often, I had other commitments. (Even after eleven years of retirement, I have not mastered the word "no".)

Because our cottage is still a work-in-progress, Frank has no trouble filling his time with woodworking projects, repair jobs, and finishes needed inside the cottage. The setting is well-treed with no close neighbours during the winter. Frank enjoys the peacefulness. He has a workshop set up in the basement. Each day, he accomplishes what he can on the Honey, Do List, interrupted only by an occasional cup of tea, before he returns home by evening meal time.

As the cottage telephone is upstairs, I have found that it's useless to call him; he seldom hears the ring. Occasionally, when he has heard it, this 68-year-old love-of-my-life would race up the outside steps, fling open the cottage door, run across the room to grab the phone, only to be greeted by a telemarketer. This having happened more than once, I think he chooses now to disregard the ring of the telephone entirely. Having a cell phone would be the perfect answer, except that our cottage area is in a "dead zone".

On this particular December day, I was preparing supper when I heard Frank's car arrive. He slammed the door upon entering the house, rattling anything not nailed down. I braced myself for "bad news" as he stomped up the stairs to the kitchen.

"Is that angry look for me? What's wrong?" I asked.

"I'm lucky to be here."

I was suddenly filled with a sick feeling. "Why? What's happened?"

"The door to my shop locked with me inside!"

I took a minute to picture Frank alone in his shop, no phone, no neighbours, no second door, and the only door refusing to budge. There were two windows, but Frank was years past the size that could wiggle out through either of them

"So, how did you get out?"

"I used the crowbar and smashed a hole in the door."

Again I paused, picturing this.

"How many swings?" I asked.

"Two!"

I knew from both the tone and the expression that this was not a time for more questions. A good supper, his newspaper, some TLC, and a prayer of thanks were in order. Later we would discuss getting an extension phone for the cottage, along with a new door and lock.

We tended to those things the very next week, although, instead of a brand new door, Frank patched the broken one. The lock was now no longer part of the knob. Instead, Frank added a padlock to the outside of the door. Because there's now an extension phone docked near his workbench, I feel more content about Frank being alone in his remote workshop.

Now let us fast forward to a spring day and add our faithful old dog, Duffy. A black and white mixture of Springer spaniel and border collie, Duffy is very protective of us and of the property. He loves to roam the cottage lot when we are there; however, when we go away for a few hours, we convert Frank's workshop into a makeshift kennel. This is not Duffy's favourite spot, but he complies.

On this spring day, although Frank had left Duffy with a full water bowl inside the locked shop, apparently Frank was away too long. When he returned, he was met by Duffy running down the cottage driveway, barking a welcome. Frank was puzzled until he saw his shop door. It was wide open with the padlock still attached, and the whole doorframe was smashed out and hanging at a strange angle.

No, Duffy had not had an accomplice. Incriminating evidence of black hairs still clung to the inside of the door. Apparently, Duffy had just kept throwing his sixty-pound body against the door until the frame gave way. It was a case of a determined dog persevering until his prison-break was accomplished.

Duffy is twelve and a half years old. According to dog-year math, that's equal to eighty-seven human years.

I would guess that we are one of the few families to be able to boast of having two "senior escape artists"!

Take Me Out To the Ball Game!

Being in the stands to see a ballgame at the Toronto Sky Dome is a treat. The getting to the Sky Dome can be a challenge, sometimes even a Believe-It-Or-Not experience. Our friends, Raymond and Ruby Bell of Foresters Falls, Ontario, can testify to that.

A few years ago, before everyone carried a cell phone, the cheerful couple drove to the outskirts of Toronto where they parked their car and hurried to catch the GO Train, a most convenient way to get to downtown Toronto. The plan was to get off at the Dome and meet their son-in-law who had tickets for the game.

The train pulled up to the platform and Raymond, stepping on, looked behind at Ruby who had hesitated.

"Come on Ruby, get on," he urged.

The words were barely out of his mouth before the doors slammed shut. The train started moving with Raymond on the inside and Ruby, outside, watching him disappear.

Another passenger, having seen the drama, kindly offered her advice to Raymond, "Don't worry, sir. See that train on the other track going the other way? At the next stop, just get off. Hurry across to the other side and get on that train. It will take you back to where your wife will be waiting."

Raymond shook his head. "You don't know my wife," he replied.

But not having a better idea, he took the woman's advice. However, he positioned himself at the window and watched the train coming the other way. Sure enough, there was

Ruby, now on the train going towards downtown Toronto! She did not see Raymond and, at this point, wondered whether she would ever see him again.

Now back at the starting point, Raymond caught the train to downtown Toronto. He and Ruby were at least pointed in the same direction this time but on separate trains. Finding each other at the Sky Dome would be a modern-day miracle.

Not knowing just where Ruby might have disembarked, Raymond got off at the end of the platform so he could walk the full distance along the building. Ruby, meanwhile, had been upstairs searching in vain for either Raymond or her son-in-law, Brian. One can only imagine her panic.

She returned to the train's platform and kept scanning the crowds arriving by train. Finally, she spotted Raymond a long distance away, walking resolutely along the platform, he, too, intently scrutinizing the swarms of people. She ran as fast as she could, pushing through the crowd until she reached him and was able to hug him tightly. What relief!

The two of them, now like Siamese twins, scouted the area looking for Brian. He had said he would meet them on the west side. Surely he had not given up and left. Raymond, using the setting sun as his guide, was positive they were on the west side. As a last resort, still hand in hand, they took a tour around the corner and there was Brian, wondering why they were so late.

"It's quite a story," said Raymond, "but let's get to the game before anything else happens!"

They had missed the first two innings of the ballgame, but this paled in comparison to what could have been. That excursion is definitely one that will never be forgotten.

You Know You Are Having a Bad Day When ...

Our daughter, Laurie, is working full time as an educational assistant while trying to complete a course that will add to her credits and eventually put more money in her pocket. This course has had many assignments and the last one was very detailed. To me it sounded like she was writing her life history! Laurie was finding it very stressful. At March Break she decided she would finish it to put an end to the misery.

It was a battle each day to concentrate on the written work while trying to ignore the beautiful sun beaming in the window. She wasn't sleeping well, her cheerful disposition was "on hold", and her head throbbed. As a single parent of two, her "breaks" were spent dealing with accumulated laundry. Because her dryer was broken, she was filling baskets with wet clothes, loading them into her car and driving the short distance to our house to use our dryer. I offered to help but she was determined to manage what she could on her own.

Finishing her morning shower on day four of March Break, she was already mentally preparing the next part of her written work. Her thoughts were scattered, jumping from project ideas to daily life: Her hair appointment would have to be cancelled. When would she have time to buy groceries? What was there in the cupboard to eat if she didn't shop? Her throat was dry and her hands were shaking even before she sat down with her books. She was beginning to hate this assignment.

To add to her troubles, her computer was at the repair shop, one more piece of broken technology. Because each day she expected it to be fixed, she had refused the loan of my computer. Surely it would be ready today. It had become a morning ritual to phone the repair shop, a number she now knew by memory, to check on whether or not the repairs had been completed.

Later, at our house as she wearily filled our dryer with the wet laundry from her house, she told me about that day's telephone episode.

"Not once, but three times, I reached a wrong number! Guess who answered the third time, Mom?" In spite of her turmoil, a smile now tugged at her lips.

I shrugged my shoulders, "Who?"

"Geriatric Mental Health, may I help you?"

I burst out laughing.

"That's exactly what I did too, Mom. It seemed almost apropos. I laughed so hard that it's a wonder the person at the other end didn't send out someone with a net to bring me in!"

"Did you find out if your computer's fixed?"

"It's not. I figure because I am being forced to do this assignment long hand, I may qualify for geriatric help by the time I'm done!"

Author's note: Laurie did finish the course. She is still sane. She smiles as she anticipates a fatter paycheque.

A Force Not to Be Reckoned With

"I'm D.D. McClure and I'm tough as nails!"

That's how the high school shop teacher introduced himself to Frank's class back in the fifties. Most of the students, especially Frank, were not impressed.

Frank must have made his feelings evident because it was obvious as the year went on that he was not Mr. McClure's favourite pupil. It could be said that they only tolerated one another.

One day, while Frank was creating a lamp on the lathe,

Mr. McClure, making his supervisory round, snarled "You're using the wrong tool! Get it out of there."

While Frank followed orders, Mr. McClure grabbed what he deemed the correct tool, and forcefully jammed it into the lathe without any explanation and without even shutting off the power. This meant that the lathe kept whirring, carving out a big ball from the wood intended for the lamp.

Centrifugal force is a powerful thing! That big ball flew right off the lathe, through the nearby window, across the parking lot outside and right through the windshield of business teacher McKelvey's car!

I think it was a toss-up that day as to whether it was teacher or student that had best learned the importance of shutting off power equipment before changing design.

Although not technically at fault, Frank never gained any "brownie points" because of this incident. It's to be hoped that D.D. McClure was as tough as he boasted because one can only imagine the conversation that must have taken place when McKelvey and McClure met later that day. No student brave enough to ask, and D.D. McClure never addressed the subject again.

Computer-Savvy

It's a rare person who has not had an embarrassing experience. Early this morning I had fired up my computer (for non-technical readers, that means I turned it on) and then went about my breakfast and news-watching routine. Later, when I tried to connect to my service provider, the local telephone company, the message box recorded the dialing and redialing, followed by the message NO ANSWER. When this happened in the past, it was usually because one of the cords connecting to the big black box (yes, that's my term for it) under my desk was loose. I checked all cords. Nothing seemed amiss.

An hour or so earlier, while I was watching the news, there had been a violent crack of lightning that had cut off the electrical power for a few seconds. Maybe this had something to do with my computer problem? Often, a sure-fire cure is to turn the computer off and then start over. I did that. Still no connection to my service provider. This meant I could continue to write stories, but could not access my e-mail or any other Internet sites.

So I added to the story I was working on. I wrote a letter.

I did a load of laundry. I cleaned out the dishwasher. In between each of these activities, I tried again to connect. Finally, I decided that perhaps the whole village was having computer-trouble, so I phoned the "communications department" of NRTCO (my service provider).

"No." No one else was reporting any problem. "Let me check at my end," Jennifer, the technical assistant, said. In less than a minute Jennifer announced, "Oh, I can see that all your lights are not lit on your modem. Is it plugged in?"

"Oh yes, I replied, it's plugged to the power bar."

"Are the lights on?"

I checked, wondering what lights I was supposed to see.

"The only light is on the very front," I said. "It's blinking."

"You have only one light on on your modem?" she asked rather incredulously. "Which light is it? What's the name beside it?"

Again, I searched the face of the black box while she waited. "There's no name and I don't see any other places that could light up."

There was silence at her end, then "Are you sure you're looking at the modem?"

"Isn't that the big box that sits under my desk?" I asked.

"Well, I'm not sure where you have it and some are bigger than others, but is it the box that you bought from us?"

Now *my* lights went on. Finally! (Some might see this as a prime example of that old saying: "The lights are on but there's nobody home.")

I knew the black box that I had been looking at had not been purchased from NRTCO. We had bought it at a computer store along with our new monitor (screen), mouse and keyboard. The black box with the lights sat just behind my left elbow, so close that I wish it had introduced itself: "Hi. I am Modem. At your service!"

I turned my head and looked at it. Definitely its lights were out, all five of them. I could feel the colour rising in my cheeks. I mumbled into the phone something like, "Oh, I'm sorry, I've been looking at the wrong box." I checked the two cords leading out from it, still wondering to myself *If this is the modem, what is that big box on the floor called?*

Sure enough, the cord that connects to the electricity was lying beneath the outlet instead of being plugged into it. Yes, that certainly had been a powerful bang earlier in the morning. Never before had I known a cord to jump right out of its outlet.

I thanked Jennifer who had been kind enough not to laugh at my ignorance.

"What is that tower-like box on the floor called?" I later asked my husband who had not been home for the morning's drama.

"Its name is 'Computer'," he said, with one eyebrow raised to show his disbelief. "That's where everything is stored."

Well, now I'm "in the know", and all you readers who are so computer-literate can stop laughing. The keyboard, the mouse, and the monitor are the only things I ever touch (except for the odd CD), but they are simply the devices that help me access the computer. Oh, and let's not forget the modem, the little black box that I have ignored for so long. I am pleased to have finally made its acquaintance!

My computer skills are akin to my driving skills. I know what to touch, push, and turn to make the car go, but I have little idea of what's happening under the hood. In times of trouble, I call a mechanic.

Easy Come, Easy Go

Kevin, our bachelor son, was in his second week of a new job. Because of the probation period that goes with any job, he was trying to put his best foot forward. His shift was 5 a.m. to 2 p.m. He routinely went to bed by 8 p.m. each night, setting the alarm for 3 a.m. This meant that every morning, he had time to make his breakfast, pack his lunch, let his dogs out, and arrive at work, ready to start at 5 a.m.

Imagine his panic the morning he woke at 4 a.m. How could this be? Had the alarm not gone off? Had he fallen back to sleep? There was no time to analyze the situation.

He pulled on some clothes and ran downstairs to his dogs that were waiting to be let out. Even though he was on a tight budget, he knew this was one day he'd have to buy both breakfast and lunch. He checked his wallet. Just as he suspected, there wasn't enough cash for two meals. Then he remembered he had a birthday card somewhere with money he hadn't spent.

Quickly rummaging through cupboards, he found his card about the same time that Mother Nature reminded him that, in his excitement, he hadn't yet gone to the bathroom. Back up the stairs he raced, money in hand.

As any male will understand, hands are needed for zippers, etc. Kevin, still in "rush mode", put the twenty-dollar bill between his teeth. Nature's mission accomplished, he flushed the toilet. After such a bodily function, one has a tendency to relax. With the clenched jaw muscle now at ease, Kevin watched in horror as the financial means to his breakfast and lunch swirled away with the last circle of water and was sucked into the abyss below.

Many expressions flashed through his mind. Ironically, he had just "wasted" his money.

"That idea's down the drain" was never truer.

E-Z Tag

This past March, in a rental car, husband Frank and I ventured away from our comfortable touring of Arizona, a State we have enjoyed for several winter holidays, to cross New Mexico and explore a bit of Texas. Our aim was to learn more history, not make history.

Things don't always go as planned.

We knew through experience that it's wise to book lodgings ahead. Having booked a motel in Houston, Texas, we were attempting to reach there before nightfall. I was the navigator; my map-reading had convinced me that the shortest route was by the Sam Houston Toll Highway. Highways may be named after historical heroes, but they are not always as reassuring as their namesakes.

Neophytes for sure, we entered this engineering wonder. It was 4:00 p.m, rush-hour traffic no matter what State you are in. In mere minutes our trip became a white-knuckled drive. Multiple lanes of traffic, vehicles travelling at terrifying speeds, cars changing lanes with little warning, and interchanges stacked three and four tiers high were challenges beyond belief. We had no idea how soon our off-ramp — on the map marked as Exit 61 — would be. Nor, did we know on which side of the road it would be. American roads use both! We were as terrified on the bottom level, looking at the interchanges stacked over our heads, as we were on the top interchange, tearing along at a death-defying speed and praying that the design of this curve would hold us in place rather than catapult us into the traffic far below.

Our View of the Stacked Interchange Loops on the Sam Houston Expressway

We knew that motorists who use a toll road pay a fee. We would gladly have done that had we been able. It was only occasionally that we saw a booth and it was always on the lane of the highway far removed from us, and certainly not Exit 61. There were signs advising us to have the exact change ready. How much was that, we wondered. Where do we pay if we simply wanted to keep going to our exit? If we swung off onto one of these ramps, would we ever be able to find our way back?

Soon we noticed that our lane had an overhead sign that said "E-Z Tag lane". Interesting. Was that a code? For what? At the speed we all were going, for us to change lanes would be to risk an accident. In fact, we wondered why there had not already been one. Or more!

Consequently, we stayed with the "E-Z Tag" travellers. I was still doing my best to read the map. According to it, Exit 61 was fast approaching. Then suddenly, I saw the exit sign. We had about three seconds to signal and get off. The highway gods must have been with us because we executed our white-knuckle escape without horns blaring or tires squealing. I was relieved, also, to see a toll gate but was surprised that the fee was only the paltry sum of $2.50. From there, we were able to find Interstate Highway #45 and our motel. How glad we were to leave this engineering wonder behind us. We knew without doubt that we would never try the Sam Houston Toll Highway again, especially at 4:00 p.m.

A few days later when visiting Cousin Monty near Houston, we mentioned our curiosity about "E-Z Tag".

"Oh, boy," he said. "Did you travel in that lane?"

"Yes, we were afraid to try to get out of it."

"Well, you can expect a fine. That lane is for drivers who have pre-paid, and they have an electronic tag on their dash to indicate they've paid. It's for people who use that highway regularly so they don't have to stop to pay each time. There's a camera set up taking pictures. Fines are issued to those having no tag. It's automatic. Likely your fine will be mailed to you."

I paled. "Do you know how much?"

"No, but it will likely be substantial."

Frank and I mulled that over, not that there was anything we could do about it now. We rather doubted that the U.S. system would find us. After all, we had rented the car from Budget Travel in Tucson, Arizona. It had California licence plates. We were to drop it at Dallas Airport, and we live in Ontario, Canada. That seemed like a lot of tracking. Probably the whole thing would be ignored.

Now, seven weeks after our holiday, our monthly MasterCard statement has arrived. There it is in black and white, a $21 charge with the word "Budget Rentals" beside it. Apparently, part of the agreement with any car rental agency is that the renter is responsible for any fines incurred and that they will automatically be charged to the credit card you used at the time of booking.

"E-Z Tag" is well-named. It seems it *is* an easy thing to tag the law-breakers!

I just thank God that Frank and I survived the experience and were able to explore Texas rather than joining Sam Houston in the "great beyond".

Sunny Side Up

Celebrations

Choir Members Sharing a Birthday Cake (Page 127)

Laurie and Philip Severin Enjoying Dish Duty at the Reunion
(Page 108)

You Never Know What Christmas Might Bring

Vi, my surrogate sister, has vivid memories of one Christmas, albeit not for the usual joyful reasons. At that time, she lived in the upper part of a duplex in Verdun, Quebec. She was content there, and happy with her landlord, Rèjean, who willingly accommodated her wishes and was conscientious about maintenance.

Attending a church service had been a long-established part of Vi's celebration of Christmas Day. Like many people in the busy Montreal area, rather than maintain an automobile, she used buses and the Metro for travelling. About ten o'clock that festive morning, she locked her apartment door, hurried down the stairs, reminded herself to lock the outer door that she shared with her landlord, and then rushed to catch the bus that would take her to church.

Returning home near the noon hour, she attempted to unlock the outside door. Try as she might, she could not make her key work in the lock. Then she remembered. Rèjean had changed the lock the day before and had told her he would give her a key. Obviously, he had forgotten. Rèjean and his family had already left to celebrate Christmas with his mother in another part of Montreal.

Shivering in the cold temperatures and wishing she had chosen a heavier coat, Vi studied her situation. The building was empty; she was on the outside in subzero temperatures; she didn't have the cell phone number for Rèjean; she didn't know the neighbours well enough to want to impose on them on Christmas Day; her thirty-year old daughter, Liette, who lived on the other side of Montreal, would not be at home right now but did plan to come and get her mother for a supper date about six p.m. Of course, she expected her mother to be inside, not here on the street! Vi, who does not have a cell phone, decided to go to the nearby Champlain Hospital and telephone Liette on the chance that she might still be at home. She was not surprised when there was no answer — she knew her daughter had earlier plans.

Vi's problem now was: Where do you go on Christmas Day to be out of the elements and free from worry? She told herself to keep calm, think of a way to pass the time for the next five or six hours and somehow arrange to keep the supper date with Liette. She remembered that although stores are not open, many movie theatres in the Montreal malls stay open on Christmas Day. With few other options, Vi decided to treat herself to a movie.

She dialed Liette's number again, this time leaving a message telling her where she was going and that she would call her again when the movie was over. She assured her that she would come back to the hospital lobby and wait. It was warm there, easy to find, and it offered a place to sit and read. As long as Liette received this message, all would be well; if not, Vi might end up signing herself in to the mental health wing!

Meanwhile, at his mother's on the other side of the city, Rèjean remembered the change of locks and his negligence in not giving Vi a key. He knew she would be going to church and he was well aware that she did not have a cell phone. He also remembered that Vi had mentioned the plan to enjoy a Christmas dinner at a restaurant with her daughter. He checked his watch. It was too late to get back to the apartment building before Vi returned from church and he did not have Liette's telephone number. He pictured Vi standing outside in the cold.

Rèjean was quite sure that Liette lived in the part of Montreal known as Longueil. Frantically he searched the telephone directory and was thankful to find her name listed there. His relief was short lived when his dialing produced only the voice of Liette's answering machine. Rèjean left a message which briefly explained the situation and provided his cell phone number. He also told her he was leaving to drive back to the apartment and would place the key under a large ceramic

Christmas angel that sat on the step. He knew the chance of Liette hearing this message was doubtful.

There seems to have been more than a ceramic angel playing a part in this story. Liette came home within fifteen minutes of Rèjean's having left the message. She immediately called his cell phone and arranged to meet him halfway at a well -known corner service station.

This story ends with Vi being rescued from the hospital lobby, Rèjean returning to his mother's for dinner, and Vi and Liette enjoying their meal that was now more a celebration of Thanksgiving than of Christmas.

Are you surprised that, try as she might, Vi cannot recall what movie she saw that afternoon?

Bacon for the Weekend

Detailed planning is required for a three day family reunion at which a hundred people are expected. Our Gunter family, from which I originated, has just finished a most enjoyable reunion in Coe Hill, Ontario. It began on Friday at noon with all-day registration and a bottomless pot of chili, and ended on Monday at noon. One hundred and twenty-six people registered.

Each of the eight members of the planning team volunteered months ahead for various responsibilities. My brother,

Allyn, and his wife, Maureen, (after conferring with adult sons, Mark and Steven, and their wives, Tammy and Paige) took on the monumental responsibility for making the breakfasts each of Saturday, Sunday and Monday mornings. That included buying the food and, because no other committee member volunteered, that job grew to buying the ingredients for each day's submarine lunches, too.

As the July reunion date came closer, Allyn and Maureen watched for the best deals on needed items. Soon they had thirty pounds of bacon in their freezer. In order that breakfast could be ready for a hundred people at seven-thirty each of the three mornings, they were advised to cook the sausages, bacon, and potatoes ahead of time and refrigerate them. It would then be a case of just warming everything up each morning. Things would be busy enough with cooking the eggs and the French toast, making the coffee and the regular toast, and cutting up fruit and keeping dishes washed.

On the Thursday afternoon before the weekend reunion, Steven, Paige, Tammy and Maureen commandeered Maureen's and Allyn's tidy kitchen about 2:00 to begin frying the thirty pounds of bacon, the sausages, and the potatoes. Mark was at his day job and Allyn was babysitting grandson, Jack. Steven and Paige had had valuable experience from both working in and managing restaurants; their expertise and organization in this whole "food endeavour" was a godsend.

But still, the job was tedious, and the small kitchen was soon very warm. Around six o'clock, after 10 pounds of fried bacon with 20 still to go, Tammy had to leave to take 7-year-old Sam to his ball game.

As always, many mothers and fathers of the young players were already in the bleachers when Tammy arrived. She joined them to watch the game and to chat. Tammy was pleasantly conversing with the mothers on either side of her when one friend wrinkled her brow, looked a little puzzled, peered around her, sniffed a bit, then turned back to Tammy.

"That's odd. I could swear I smell bacon cooking!"

Tammy's face reddened and she didn't know whether to laugh or cry. "That bacon smell is me!" she announced. To her now thoroughly perplexed friends, she explained about the bacon-cooking marathon from which she had just made her temporary escape, and how there had been no time to change clothes.

Everyone had a good laugh.

"No sense changing your clothes if you have to return to that kitchen," one friend said. "Though you *are* making me hungry!"

Meanwhile, the pounds of bacon were slowly being made edible, along with the sausages and potatoes. By eleven that night, everything had been cooked and refrigerated, and sleep was the order.

Sometimes sleep is more easily ordered than accomplished. About three in the morning, Maureen was so restless that she decided to get up. To her surprise, she found son Steven sitting in the kitchen, he, too, unable to sleep. As they talked, great numbers of mosquitoes began joining them. How odd to have such a bunch of them in the kitchen! Where were they coming from?

Steven and Maureen began checking windows and screens. Downstairs in the rec room they discovered one window screen absolutely covered in mosquitoes. Closer investigation revealed a small hole in that screen. The smell of the bacon had attracted hordes of these pests and entrance had been gained. From there, it was only a matter of minutes until they appeared in the kitchen, the source of this delectable smell. It would seem that mosquitoes love pork as much as they love human flesh.

A spray was used to eliminate those still on the outside and a bit of tape patched the hole. Nothing much could be done about the pests already inside.

Because Allyn and Maureen took a well-deserved extended holiday after the reunion, it was a week before they returned to their house. Happily, there was neither any telltale cooking smell nor buzzing insects. Even though the smell is gone, for Allyn, Maureen and their family, the memories of "the breakfast brigade" will undoubtedly last forever.

"Three of the Reunion Cooks"
Paige, Steven, Mark Gunter

Barely Seventy

Last night for the first time since I was the child who didn't want to make the trek to the outdoor toilet, I slept with a pot under my bed. The difference was that it was a cooking pot, not a chamber pot. In fact, it was the pot, the lid, and a large spoon.

Yesterday, June 17, 2009, was my husband Frank's seventieth birthday. Because we'd already marked this happy occasion by a family celebration on the weekend, Frank and I were observing the actual birth date with a simple, quiet time, just the two of us, at the cottage. Earlier in the day, I had baked his favourite, Queen Elizabeth cake. At lunchtime, I topped it with seven candles, one for each decade. I even took a picture.

About six o'clock I put two marinated steaks on the outdoor barbeque in preparation of our evening meal. Soon we sat down indoors at the kitchen table to enjoy these, away from the mosquitoes. We were almost finished when I remarked that I'd better make us some tea. I walked to the sink with the kettle and then froze, kettle in hand. No, I wasn't having a stroke. Through our window over the sink, I was looking at a bear - a big black bear! It was ambling its way across our back lawn, toward me, headed for the back door that's about two feet away from the window.

"Frank. There's a bear," I whispered, my mouth so dry I could hardly form the words.

He jumped up from the table to look. His words, although spoken quietly, were a little more vivid than "oh dear".

In the thirty-odd years that we had owned this property, we'd never encountered a bear here. We watched, both fascinated and scared, as the bear crossed over to the steps at our back door and glided down three of them to the tall, black, plastic composter. Then he proceeded to lift off the lid, toss it aside, and help himself to a chunk of bread. I say "he" because we have no idea whether this was Mama or Papa.

I ran to the side patio doors to look for Duffy, our dog; he was stretched out near the barbeque. He's a border-collie–springer-spaniel mix, but old and deaf, and almost blind. I managed to get him into the cottage by offering him part of the birthday supper, quietly thankful he had not smelled the bear. Then I grabbed my camera.

I had lots of time as it turned out. Our visitor was not in a hurry; he took his bread to a comfy spot on the lawn, ate it and then returned to the composter for more. We watched his repeated trips, noting that he was sampling anything edible, including eggshells. Frank and I talked in whispers; I snapped lots of photos from the safety of the glass in our back door.

Finally "Bruin" had exhausted the supply of composter treats, leaving behind only the grass and leaves. As he headed for the woods, it looked like he was leaving, but then he seemed to change his mind as he started our way again.

That's when Frank suggested maybe we'd better phone a neighbour. At the same time, he pulled the heavy drapes over the patio glass doors, shutting out the view of us from our unwanted guest should the bear decide to visit the deck on that side of the cottage.

Our cottage is in rather a remote location and we knew, so far, that none of our immediate neighbours had opened up their cottages yet. We were whispering about whom to phone when something black moved on the patio deck. We still had a view through a window on that side. Yes, Bruin was there, now investigating the barbeque. Frank and I huddled together on the other side of the room. We figured that one lunge by Bruin against the glass doors would probably gain him entry.

I grabbed the telephone book and portable phone. I was shaking so badly I could hardly turn the pages. I called the number of a friend who lived about five minutes by car from us. Busy signal! Darn! I did know their neighbours, Pierre and Pierrette, but on a first-name-only basis. God must have been looking after us because *Colbert*, their last name, now popped into my head. When Pierrette answered on the first ring, I talked breathlessly, trying to tell her about our visitor and our fright. She gave the phone to Pierre and I handed ours to Frank. I had decided that this was a man-problem. I cannot remember any of the conversation, only Frank's assuring me, after he'd hung up, that help was on the way. Bruin had now left the deck but we had no idea where he'd gone.

Twenty minutes of more watching, waiting and planning went by. Our game plan was that we would run to our vehicle if the bear made its way into the cottage. Hopefully, Duffy would follow us. In hindsight, it might have been safer to have shut Duffy in the bathroom.

In this twenty minutes, Bruin returned to the deck and checked the warm barbeque once more. Then he ambled down the steps and disappeared from view again. Shortly after this, our friend Pierre, along with his friends, Frank and Ruth Miller, drove into the driveway. Frank Miller is retired from the military and has a licensed gun, a 30-06. I felt so much safer just seeing that gun.

He and Pierre scouted the property while the rest of us viewed the pictures on my digital camera and talked about how big and bold Bruin was.

We invited our rescuers inside to share tea and birthday cake. This had turned out to be more of a party than we had anticipated. The gun was ready and waiting to scare the "party crasher" should Bruin appear again. Thankfully, he never did.

With our would-be rescuers gone, Frank and I debated against staying the night but it was getting late and packing up would be a tiring task. We decided to go to bed armed. That's when I stashed the cooking pot, lid, and large spoon under the bed. Bruin would be serenaded with one awful racket if he returned.

Surprisingly, we both slept soundly. I guess we were exhausted by the high anxiety of the evening.

First thing next morning, I phoned the Ministry of Natural Resources to tell them the story of the strangest seventieth birthday celebration ever. They patiently and politely explained to me all the things we had done incorrectly. I appreciate their advice but I'm not sure I could ever yell at the bear and tell it to go away when it's close enough to leave its breath fog on our patio door!

Upon relating this bear story to Artis Williams, a BC cousin of mine who is a bit older, I was surprised that she did not show any concern. I guess my story pales in comparison with her experience. She told me that a large bear had visited them at their country home, entering a back verandah where they kept their deep freeze. The bear had opened the lid and literally cleaned out all the meat. She and husband, Ed, reflecting on this incident, had decided that the verandah was a poor place to have their freezer and so did not immediately replenish the supply. They cleaned everything out of it out but temporarily left it sitting there.

A few days later, as Artis was napping on the verandah's couch, the bear made a second visit. Artis awoke to see the bear, freezer lid now up, climbing over the edge and into the empty freezer. She realizes now, had she been thinking, she could probably have shut the lid and trapped it there. Instead, she grabbed the bear-banger, a device Ed had

A bear-banger like the one used by Artis to scare the bear away

made for her, and pulled the firing knob on it so hard that the noise scared her as well as the bear. The bear scrambled out and ran, never to return. What a brave lady! She says that while not welcomed onto the verandah, bears are a common sight in her area. I hope I never can say that!

Things We Have Learned about Deterring Bears:

1. Bears can smell eggs shells miles away and love them. Don't add them to your cottage composter.

2. Turn your compost often so there is little odour. Fruit attracts bears.

3. Cover the top layer with newspaper (keeps the odour down

and will become part of the compost).

4. Wear a bell or talk loudly when in the woods so as not to startle a bear.

5. If a bear invades your space, bang pots and pans, make loud noises, blow a whistle, scream at it, do anything to make it uncomfortable. If you let it make itself at home, it will keep coming back. (Oh, no!).

6. Bears come into populated areas only when nature does not provide enough food. Except for mothers with cubs, who feel threatened, they seldom attack humans.

7. Do not turn and run from a bear. Back away slowly and leave it alone. (Try #5 advice.)

8. Don't continue to fill your bird feeder once spring has arrived. Hungry bears are attracted to it, too.

Author's personal note: Numbers 1, 2, 3, 4 and 8 are easy. Numbers 5 and 7 will take practice, and I am hoping I never have to test myself!

Surprise! Surprise!

Milestone birthday celebrations are fun, especially if they can be kept as a surprise for the one being honoured. This was the case when my good friend, Vi L'Esperance's seventieth birthday was approaching.

Liette, Vi's daughter, started the organizing several months ahead of the June 25th birthday. An invitation was sent by e-mail to people like me and by telephone to other long-time friends. Liette had heard her mother mention some new acquaintances but, having lived in her own apartment for at least fifteen years, she had met only a few of them. Liette had no idea of last names, addresses or phone numbers, and she knew, if she quizzed her mother, that her mother would become suspicious.

A bit of deceit is sometimes needed. Liette called her mother to say that she was coming over for a visit. After chatting for a while in the living room, she suggested they go out for dinner.

"Go freshen up, Mom. I'll do some book work I brought with me."

As soon as Vi had closed the bathroom door, Liette grabbed her mother's address book from beside the phone. Then she headed to the kitchen table and began flipping the pages, looking for names she'd heard Vi talking about. She had to rely on first names only, hoping they were the right friends. She scribbled these quickly into her own little book, along with the phone numbers. All the while that Liette was transferring names and numbers, Vi was moving back and forth between the bedroom and the bathroom.

"I'll take a sweater in case the air-conditioning is on, okay?"

"Sounds good, Mom."

"I trust you're getting well paid for all these extra hours you put in for your boss."

"Me, too."

Liette, only half-listening, hoped she was giving the correct answers. Finishing the pilfering, she returned the address book to its rightful place. The next day she started phoning.

I arrived by bus on Thursday evening and Vi met me at the terminal, pleased that I had come for a visit. Since I make this a habit about three times a year, often at her birthday time, she did not suspect any other plan might be in the making. She mentioned that Liette would be picking us up for dinner Sunday night.

"I think my friend Carol Anne is planning to meet us at the restaurant. I've been wanting you to meet her. Liette says the four of us will celebrate my birthday."

"Oh, good. It'll be nice to put a face with Carol Anne's name."

****

On Sunday afternoon about the same time as Vi and I were getting dressed for what Vi thought was a foursome dinner date, Liette was stuffing helium-filled balloons into her small, compact car, tying them down and hoping there was still enough room for the two ladies she was to pick up en route to the restaurant. She did get the load transported safely, but told me afterwards she could scarcely see a thing in her rear view mirror.

Meantime, Carol Anne phoned us and suggested she'd pick us up. Actually this was part of Liette's plan, but it was to sound like an idea that Carol Anne had suddenly hatched. No doubt about it, deceit is a key factor in any surprise party.

After an hour's drive across Montreal, we arrived at the Japanese restaurant that Liette had booked for the party. Nothing looked unusual, although Vi did wonder where Liette was. We asked for the L'Esperance reservation and the waiter ushered us into another room where ten women screamed "Surprise" as loudly as they could.

Vi's face showed total disbelief. Because the lights were very low, she took a couple more steps ahead so she could inspect the faces. "You all knew about this and no one told me?" she exclaimed to her laughing friends.

"How else would we have been able to have a surprise party!" one of them retorted, obviously pleased with their accomplishment.

A bouquet of seven huge, pastel-coloured helium balloons, one for each decade of her life, was attached to the chair designated for Vi. In front of her was an elegant centerpiece of red roses and white mums, a gift from one of the guests. More gifts, waiting to be opened after the meal, were piled on another table.

When our dinner orders were delivered, each one a Japanese specialty, we delighted in the finesse with which our food was displayed on the plate. Not only did it taste good, it looked almost too ele-gant to disturb, a real work of art.

Vi admires her birthday gifts as friend Doris Worth looks on.

The passing hours were filled with visiting, toasting, eating, picture-taking, gift-opening, and laughter. Finally we prepared to leave. Even though the sun had set, the evening sky was streaked with pinks, blues, yellows, and mauves that accentuated the birthday balloons Vi was clutching. Carefully, we carried the gifts to the open trunk of Liette's car. Vi waited patiently, holding the balloons until the last gift was in place, then she proceeded to push the balloons into the trunk while Liette kept her hand on the trunk lid.

The rest of us were standing nearby saying our good byes. Suddenly there was a scream from Vi. We all turned in her direction in time to see the balloons floating above the trunk and ascending higher and higher, quite out of reach, making their way to join the pastel-patterned sky.

"Well … It's a good thing this happened now and not before the party," Liette said.

"How stupid of me! Liette, I'm so sorry. I guess I just let go of them," Vi berated herself.

"It's okay, Mom. You wouldn't believe the pain I went through trying to drive here with those in the car. Now we don't have to worry about them any more at all."

We all laughed heartily at this bit of wisdom. Some of us wondered where the balloons would land and what lucky person might find them. Maybe we'd read about it in the newspaper!

It certainly was a unique but appropriate way to end the party: the symbolic seven decades had just floated away. Who wants to be reminded of a number of years? It's the good memories that count.

The Purr-fect Twenty-fifth

Twenty-five years of marriage is a milestone that should be recognized. Sometimes the question is how to celebrate with friends and family without it all becoming too formal. A perfect solution is to hold the party at your house and pitch a large dining tent or two in the backyard. That's what friends of our daughter did recently.

Invitations, designed and printed by the couple, were sent out to nearly one hundred people. Although close friends helped with food preparation, much of it was done by the happy couple and their children. The day before the party they made twelve dozen cupcakes and were glad of nearby neighbours who had extra room in their refrigerators.

Our son-in-law was appointed the main barbeque chef. Hamburgers, hot dogs, and salads galore were the order of the day. A dessert buffet was set up inside the house. The crowning touch was a large chocolate fondue, the kind that is triple-tiered with ongoing cascades of oozing brown chocolate. Guests could select their choice of fruit from strawberries, pineapple, cherries, and bananas, thread these onto a skewer, and then rotate them under the chocolate falls. Some guests were happy just to watch the beauty of it all.

Add to that group, the resident cat, Aisha. Anyone who claims they own a cat is mistaken. True cat lovers recognize that a cat is definitely "the owner" of the house. It rules. Aisha was on the prowl, checking out intruders, and then returning to her perch on the banister near the cascading chocolate, all the while, switching her tail. Our granddaughter suggested to some family members that maybe Aisha should be corralled in a bedroom — the buffet, especially the constant rippling chocolate, might prove too tempting. She was assured that Aisha never bothered with the food. It would be unheard of for anything like that to happen.

Not wanting to be a party-pooper, my granddaughter said nothing when she later noticed Aisha sporting a somewhat chocolate-covered tail. By then the house and yard were full of happy revellers and she hoped no one would notice. Aisha could continue to rule. She, herself, would pass on the chocolate fondue.

Whose Turn Is It?

It's a rare person who doesn't enjoy a birthday party, especially, as we get older, if it's for someone else.

I'm the organist and choir leader of a small but faithful United Church choir in the little village of Foresters Falls. Our practices are Thursday evenings. Once a month, after practice, we hurry next door to Margaret Curry's, the retired organist's, for a party. So far we have never had a month that some choir member did not have a birthday.

Margaret has the tea made (hers always tastes better than anyone else's), the plates out, and candles ready. One of the choir members supplies the ice cream and another brings the homemade cake. It's never the same kind two months in a row. We never know whether it will be chocolate, Black Forest, lemon, spice, marble, or the recipe called "hummingbird". We just know there will be a cake and it will be delicious. Forget about calories.

Well … That's usually the case. One time, not too long ago, we were all gathered at Margaret's for the celebration of three birthdays: Eleanor Black's, Catherine Bromell's, and Lillis Hawthorne's. We have a second Eleanor in our choir, Eleanor Waite, and she was still at the church.

"What's taking Eleanor so long?" Margaret asked. "She's supposed to bring the cake."

"She said she had to put some things away but she'd be right over," someone said.

Shortly after, Eleanor did arrive. We noted that she was not carrying any cake.

"Did you not bring a cake?" Margaret asked.

"No," she announced, completely surprised by the question. "Did I say I would bring it this month?"

She knew by our burst of laughter that the answer was yes.

"This has to be a first! A cake-less birthday party!" one of our members quipped.

That might have been the case had it not been for "Margaret to the rescue". Without saying a thing she made her way to her deep-freeze. From it she produced two McCain's frozen chocolate cakes, the little rectangular flat kind. A quick trip through the microwave and voila! Cake for the party!

While Margaret was tending to this, Eleanor was regaling us with the saga of The Cake That Could Have Been. A huge slab cake with the three birthday girls' names was sitting at home in her freezer. It had been there for a month or more and she had forgotten all about it. Eleanor, a very busy and very creative person, is often hired to make and decorate cakes for special occasions in and around the village. That cake had originally been baked and decorated for a birthday party for "Aunt Myrtle". Eleanor had etched the words 'Happy Birthday Aunt Myrtle" in icing across the beautifully decorated cake. Unfortunately that party had to be cancelled. Eleanor scraped off the inscription and changed it to Lillis, Catherine, and Eleanor, ready ahead of time for the next choir party. Into the freezer it went, *out of sight, out of mind,* as the saying goes. Now it was too late to thaw that much cake, so McCain's would have to suffice.

Wishes were made, candles blown out, and the usual fun and visiting continued with only a giggle now and then about the "forgotten cake". In fact, the memory of it has provided us with lots of laughter and Eleanor has received her share of good-natured ribbing. She tells me that at a later date, the family was able to have Aunt Myrtle's birthday and so Eleanor scraped and redid the inscription again, this time remembering to deliver the cake to the party on time.

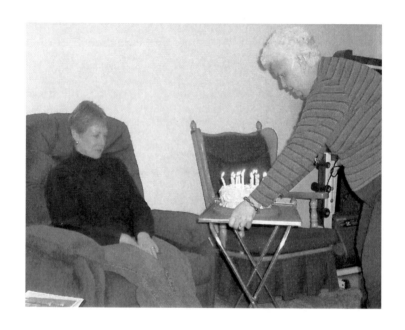

One of Many Choir Parties
(Marilyn Coughlin & Eleanor Waite)

Creatures,
Loved and Unloved

Cute Puppy George (Page 134)

Heather Campbell

Who's The Master of the House?

What do you buy your bachelor son for his birthday? Anything and everything, the more practical the better.

Besides the usual gift of money, I had bought him tea towels, oven mitts, and a roast of beef along with the slow-cooker recipe and the packaged soup mix to go with it. I had frozen the roast and delivered it in a cooler.

Kevin put this roast into his freezer to save for a day when his shift work made meal preparation difficult.

A few weeks later, when checking my answering machine, I heard Kevin's voice. "Thanks for the roast, Mom. It was good but you might want to tell people to never put a roast in a slow cooker and then go to bed when you have a German Shepherd Dog in the house."

Immediately I pictured the roast having been pulled onto the floor and devoured by this beautiful canine named Camille, the pet that Kevin had had for only a few months.

But Kevin was laughing. "Mom," he went on. "About every hour and a half, Camille's howling woke me up. The first couple of times I got up and went downstairs to see what was wrong. There she sat, as calmly and as obediently as she could look, staring up at the crock pot. Then she'd start to wag her tail,

133

sure I was going to feed her. 'No, Camille,' I told her. 'Lie down and be quiet.' She would look dejected but she'd obey.

I'd go back upstairs but it wouldn't be long before the howling would begin again and we'd go through the same performance. That roast of beef did smell good.

The third time I came downstairs to put an end to it. I knew I had to change tactics. I got some dog biscuits, stretched out on the chesterfield, and put the biscuits on the floor for Camille, and then told her to lie down there. I put my hand on her head and soon we both went to sleep. I guess I might have had four hours sleep in total that night before the alarm rang. By now the smell was sure tempting me too. I tied Camille outside in her yard, gave her the usual daily rations, promising her some beef-flavoured biscuits soon, and hurried back inside. I guess you could say that I was ready to sample a roast that was dog-gone good!"

Bolted

Having a passionate interest in a hobby adds to the joy of life, as does the love of dogs. Sometimes putting these two things together can cause a problem.

Our son, Kevin, approaching mid-life, has been a lover of motor vehicles since he was old enough to hold a matchbox-size model in his hand. From the early days of changing the design of these models (often with the unapproved use of his father's hacksaw), to the teenage years when he concentrated on the speed and engine power of motorbikes, his favourite place has been the garage. Now he is a qualified automotive technician and an amateur stock car builder and driver. All his spare time — not to mention all his extra cash — is focused toward modifying, racing, and repairing his stock car.

That's why, a week ago, he was working feverishly in his garage, replacing his stock car's worn shocks before the weekend race. At his heels was George, a fourteen-week old German Shepherd pup, the newest addition to the household. Kevin loves dogs almost as much as he loves motors, which explains why George is now one of three dogs who try to make themselves fit into Kevin's bachelor-size house.

Absorbed in his work, as Kevin removed each shock, he put the corresponding bolts on the floor within easy reach for use with the new shocks. Then confidently, he began the replacement. Ready for the last bolt, his hand and his eye went to the floor simultaneously. In disbelief, he saw there was no bolt. How could that be? Then he realized there was also no George.

Calling George, Kevin quickly stepped outside to look.

There was George, just out of reach, with the bolt hanging from his mouth. As soon as he saw Kevin, he wagged his tail and ran in the opposite direction. Then he put the bolt down, looked back at Kevin, and waited for him to come for it. As soon as Kevin got within arm's distance from him, George would grab his prize and bolt away again (pun intended). Kevin has a huge yard and it soon became apparent that George loved this game. This was even better than the stick-fetching Kevin had been teaching him.

Only a dog-lover like Kevin would be able to enjoy the game, too, and not become upset that a fourteen-week-old pup obviously had the upper hand (in this case, paw) and was leading him on a merry chase.

As Kevin told us later, "It was at least fifteen minutes before George slowed down enough that I could catch him. How *shocking* is that?"

The new shocks have now been installed and many more repairs done since, but George is no longer apprenticing in Kevin's garage.

Down by the Bay

You may know the song that starts "Down by the bay (echo), where the watermelons grow (echo) ..." — the one in which you call on someone in the audience to supply the line: "Did you ever see a ..." (example, did you ever see a goat with a purple raincoat), and then everyone joins in to sing the line "down by the bay". Any camp group, especially young people, love these "zipper songs", as they are called.

Next time you have to fill in this line, you might use something from Frank's tale of a sight he witnessed a few years ago at the farm of Mr. McLeod who lives on the Town Line just outside Cobden. As on many farms, there was a tall corn silo. Corn is dumped into the top and stored for food for the cattle. The liquid that's a natural result of this process, drains into a reservoir at the bottom of the silo.

When Frank drove into the farmyard one warm summer day, he passed cows standing in whatever shade they could find in the open pasture, a few horses huddling together near the fence, and near the silo, he saw what could only be called "a hen party". Hens were literally teetering from one leg to another, rushing ahead a few steps and then staggering sideways, heads pivoting, wings making half-mast efforts. In the middle of it all was the rooster who had lost control of his harem; he was doing his best to crow, but try as he might by stretching his neck and tilting his head at various angles, no cock-a-doodle do would come from that dandy's throat. His "song" sounded more like a hiccup.

Frank wasn't long in figuring out that the whole group was drunk! As Mr. McLeod later explained, the corn liquid in the reservoir had fermented. The bawdy henhouse gang had discovered the "open bar" and, as with any good corn liquor, inebriation was taking its toll.

"Did you ever see a chicken, corn liquor a'lickin'...down by the bay?"

Man's Best Friend

Frank, having worked for various civil engineering firms, has made the acquaintance of many interesting characters and situations. He tells what could be termed a "dog-gone-good" story that happened on a construction job where trucks transported crushed gravel from the crusher site to the stockpile.

Each truck would pull up to the crusher's conveyor belt, stop, the driver would get out and turn on the belt until the truck was loaded. Then the driver would shut off the belt, climb back into the truck, then pull ahead onto the road. By that time there would be another truck behind to do the same thing.

Paul, one of the drivers, always took his faithful little dog, Corky, in his cab. Corky was a cute black-and-white terrier that spent the whole of every working day sitting on the passenger seat.

One particular day, Bill (one of the other drivers), after having admired Corky and talking to him through the window as Paul's truck was loading, suggested, "Why don't I take Corky with me on this next run? I love dogs."

"Sure, if you want, but don't get too attached," Paul laughed. He then picked up Corky, took him to Bill's truck, and placed him lovingly on the seat beside Bill. He closed the truck door and waved good-bye. Paul then waited behind the other trucks for his turn to pull under the chute to receive his load.

Meanwhile, Bill had reached the weigh scale where he had to get out of his truck to get the ticket required for each truck. When he took the few steps back to open the truck door, he was greeted by a fierce canine face that had turned from friend to foe! Corky's fangs were showing, his growl was murderous, and his bark warned Bill to "get back!" Bill attempted to humour, cajole, even plead, but Corky was not letting him into that truck. This was not Paul. This was a stranger.

The minutes were accumulating as were the trucks lining up behind Bill's. A supervisor appeared on the scene to see why the trucks had stopped moving.

"How much is that doggie in the window?" were not the words that roared from his lips. In fact, the exact words are probably better left to one's imagination.

Back at the conveyor belt, Paul was just leaving with his load. As he approached the line of trucks at the weigh station, twelve in all, he noted that nothing was moving! What had happened? Then he saw Carl, the supervisor, storming his way.

Carl was livid. His rant on "guard dog Corky" and the loss of expensive time that he was causing was electrifying, to say the least.

Paul, not daring to laugh, hurried down from his truck cab, then actually ran to keep pace with the aggravated supervisor as they made their way back to the scene of the "hold-up".

As soon as Corky saw Paul, his little tail began wagging, and he pressed his paws against the window pane, waiting to be rescued by his master. That "rescue" ended a tense scene and Bill was able to enter his own truck.

Paul, with Corky under his arm, hurried back to his truck and, one by one, the trucks were able to move ahead.

The truck drivers, now all fully aware of what the problem had been, honked their horns in applause as Bill left the weigh scales. Bill, joining in the fun, waved his hand, but he was glad none of them could see how red his face was.

The Rescue

"What is that?"

"What's what?" Frank asked, looking up from his magazine.

"That!" I pointed, annoyed that he had not noticed the plump, black bump on our new rec room carpet.

I bent over, extending my index finger toward the blob.

Suddenly I shrieked, raced across the family room, jumped onto the chesterfield beside Frank, screaming, "It moved! It moved! Oh God, it moved!"

I dug my nails into Frank's arm, trembling in terror, and tramping over the cushions as I tucked myself in behind him, screaming one second and whimpering the next. Frank attempted to stand up. This sent me into a worse state of panic. I dove off the chesterfield and headed for the stairway, afraid any minute the "thing" would scurry under my feet. Out of the corner of my eye, as I sprinted up the stairs, I saw Frank reaching for the shovel and poker from beside the woodstove.

At the top of the stairs, I slammed the door behind me, taking refuge in the kitchen, glad to be able to hug Duffy, our faithful old spaniel.

My heart pounded until I heard Frank opening the stove door. "Oh, good! He's rid of it!" I said to Duffy, wondering at the same time why I was so paranoid about mice and bats.

I heard Frank coming up the stairs. He opened the door and smiled.

"It's gone?" I gulped.

"Yes honey. That threatening, vile chunk of Duffy's black hair will never bother you again!"

The Watchdog and "The Rocket"

Any large dog commands a certain amount of respect. Our son Kevin lives alone, except for his two German Shepherd Dogs, George and Jessie. He loves dogs, both for companionship and for protection. Jessie was still a pup but George was 4 years old, large and powerful and well-trained as a watchdog. Frank and I are nervous of him.

When Kevin is at home, both dogs are in the house except for the times he walks them.

One Tuesday in late August, Frank — driving his old 1991 Honda Civic, the one we fondly but erroneously call "The Rocket" — visited Kevin. The dogs, of course, were in the house. George, penned in his crate in the kitchen, set up a terrible ruckus and would not stop barking at Frank. Frank continued to calmly smoke a cigarette (Kevin does not smoke) and, determining that no dog would dictate to him, thought he could stare George down. George persisted in barking and growling until Kevin, realizing the futility of the situation, suggested that he and his dad should go outside to enjoy a cup of tea. Frank has never encountered a dog that acts like George (our dogs are friendly with everyone) and muttered something about how he'd have a dog like George put down. Kevin, with teapot in hand, ushered his dad outside and George calmed down.

The rest of the visit was enjoyed outside on the deck. Frank remarked that he still had a two-hour drive ahead of him, said goodbye to Kevin and headed off. Unfortunately, before he made it home to Beachburg, "The Rocket" broke down. Frank called CAA and me. CAA towed the car to Kevin's and I

CAA to the rescue!

brought Frank home in my car.

Kevin is a well-experienced, certified auto technician. Affectionately referring to him as "Doctor Campbell" because of his keen ability to diagnose any car's ailment, we prefer to have him tend to our ill vehicles whenever possible. We would manage with my car until Kevin could fix the Honda. He has another job, but is able to squeeze the repair of our auto calamities into his life when necessary.

A week after "The Rocket's" breakdown, Kevin called to tell me that yesterday he had finally pushed the car into his garage so he could work on it today. George is on a chain near the garage but Kevin had never anticipated that he was within striking distance. He has never before caused any trouble with automobiles. However, this is Frank's car, the guy that stared at George, and had even vocalized that he didn't like him.

George, obviously, had not forgotten who owned this car. When Kevin took a look at it that day, George had eaten a hole in the bumper and had completely destroyed the mud flaps.

Kevin will replace the mud flaps but he thinks he'll just cover up the hole in the bumper with a large German Shepherd Dog picture and add the words "Don't mess with me!"

Reflections

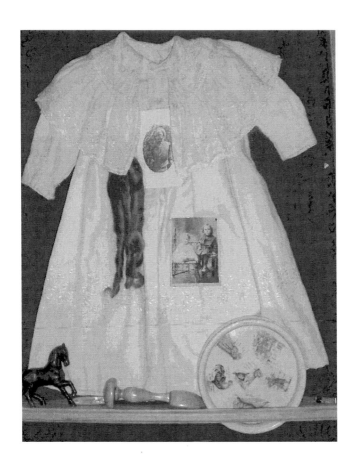

Treasures in the Shadow Box (Page 150)

Tea Cozies

Every once in a while, even though I feel great and people are kind enough to tell me, "You look so *young*", I am abruptly brought face to face with the fact that I am old.

One of those moments happened recently while I was enjoying the television quiz program *Who Wants to Be a Millionaire?* I like to play along, testing my knowledge. The first five questions that must be answered correctly so the contestant will not go home empty-handed (which has happened) are relatively easy. There are four answers provided for each question, from which the contestant must pick the one that is correct. On this particular day, the young lady (probably mid-twenties) had not even hesitated on the first three questions but on the next one she was completely puzzled and admitted "I have no idea!"

The question was "What is a tea cozy?" Of the four suggested answers, "teapot cover" was clearly the choice but, because she had no knowledge of tea cozies, she decided to use a "Lifeline". Each contestant has the option of three Lifelines: Phone a Friend, Ask the Audience or ask for the 50/50 whereby two of the four answers are eliminated. There must have been enough people in the audience that were my age or older because, when she chose their help, about eighty percent knew what a tea cozy is.

In my house, I have two tea cozies. I also have one at the cottage. My mother knit all three of them. I often saw the teapot in my parents' home all snug in its multi-coloured cozy. We always knew the tea would still be hot even if we were tardy serving it.

A few years ago when our granddaughters, Amanda and Jessica, were having a winter holiday at the cottage and wanted to go sliding, Amanda realized she had not brought any type of hat. What do you supposed she used as a substitute? The seldom-used tea cozy fit her head perfectly. I expect if she had been going to a ski hill, she might have scorned it. But our cottage is well off the beaten track and she was more concerned about being warm than about being fashionable.

Although I have them, I must admit that I rarely use tea cozies on my teapots. They are in the drawer with the tea towels and that's where they stay. Maybe it's because life moves at such a fast pace now. Because we seldom linger over a meal, the tea really doesn't have a chance to become cold.

Today, many young people do not drink tea. Those who do are like our bachelor son who simply deposits a tea bag and some boiling water into a mug.

Granddaughters Amanda and Jessica
Note Amanda's tea cozy toque on the left.

Restaurant service might bring you the pot of hot water and the tea bag but from there on, it's the customer's responsibility. Can you imagine the reaction if I were to ask for a tea cozy?

All in all, once I had analyzed the whole "millionaire contest" situation, I realized that this young contestant was just that — young — not ignorant. I, on the other hand, was painfully aware of why I could have aced that question!

Sentimental Attachment

A large shadow box mounted in our hallway showcases several items that were my father's: his baby coat, his baby plate, an iron bank in the shape of a horse, one of his tie clips, and three blond ringlets. Each article, most of which are close to a hundred years old, has a story in itself, but the most interesting to me is the story associated with the ringlets.

These ringlets measure about ten inches each in length and date back to 1917, the year Dad started school. With his hair combed into perfect ringlets, and attired in a lovely brown corduroy suit sent to him by a city aunt, his mom (my grandmother) sent him off to the one-room country school. Dad was the oldest of her four children and I am sure Grandma choked back a tear as she watched her first born trudging down the hill to meet the neighbourhood children who would see that he reached school safely.

All day she awaited his return, anxious to hear about his first day at school. Unfortunately, Dad had a sad tale to tell. He arrived home quite upset because the older girls had laughed at him saying, "And what have we here, a little boy or a little girl?" They kept the teasing up every chance they got that day. Dad did not want to go back to school.

As much as it broke Grandma's heart, she knew she would have to cut off his beautiful thick hair. So the deed was done. From the severed locks, Grandma saved three of those ringlets, wrapped them in soft brown paper, and stored them away. No more ringlets and no more fancy clothes for school.

Twenty-six years later, shortly after Dad and Mom were married, Grandma gave the package of ringlets to Mom, telling her the story that went with it. I'm not sure what Mom thought of this gift at the time. It was at least another forty years before I found the package on a closet shelf when I was helping Mom and Dad pack for a move. I was thrilled with the ringlets, so Mom said I could have the treasure.

I used to think that the word "heirloom" referred to an item that was old, had family connections, and was worth a large sum of money because of its age. Many, I know, do fit that description. Others, as in my case, are treasured more for their sentimental value and family history than for what they might command at market price.

(The above memoir earned 2nd prize in the Whitewater Historical Society's 2009 contest. A slightly different version appeared in "The Show Must Go On", published in 2003).

Mice Phobia

I can detect the smell of a dead mouse better than any cat can. Of course, judging from the way our cat loves the stalking, the pouncing, and then the playing with of her injured mouse, I suppose a cat is not interested in a *dead* mouse. I sleuth out the critter and get rid of it, and its rotten smell, with as little ceremony as possible.

Getting rid of a mouse that is dead and decaying in some corner is a task I can handle. A live mouse or even a mouse in a trap is another story. To say I "freak out" is an understatement.

Yesterday, I opened the cupboard under the sink and staring back at me, its head gripped in the trap I had set there, were the beady eyes of a mouse. I slammed the door. My heart pounded. My hands turned sweaty. The mouse would have to stay there until Frank — or a braver person than I — could pick up the trap, walk it to the outdoors or to the nearest garbage receptacle, press the release, and watch it drop.

I have reasoned with myself about the silliness of this fear but, apparently, I need psychological help to conquer it.

My first memory of a mouse is very clear. I was about 6 years old and my daily job was to set the table. I had carefully placed the plates on the table and then walked to the cutlery drawer of our kitchen cupboards as I did every day to get the silverware. But this time when I pulled open the drawer, a mouse scurried out, ran across the front of the drawer and scurried away. To this day, I have no idea where it went because I could not stop screaming. Its appearance had been so unexpected and so close to my hand that I went into shock.

My screaming brought Dad onto the scene. Apparently he asked me what was wrong.

I continued to scream and point but was incapable of forming any words.

I was vaguely aware of his order "Stop screaming this minute!" but until I felt the stinging slap on my face I was unable to stop.

My father, a gentle man, had never slapped me before so, obviously, I had needed it to stop my hysteria. He told me later that he didn't know what else to do.

Of course, he'd had no idea why I was screaming. The mouse had left the premises. There was nothing sinister lurking where I was pointing. One would think I had taken leave of my senses.

Our house was much like everyone else's in the village: an attic overhead, a cellar underneath, and lots of drafty windows. I guess that made plenty of avenues for mice looking for warm nests, and crumbs left behind by unsuspecting humans.

Even in today's airtight houses, mice invade. I have climbed on chairs, vacated the room, and I've even shut myself in another room while Frank dealt with a mouse. I apologize to all my readers who are animal lovers, some to the point that they trap mice and return them to the wild. A slithering snake is not a problem. I have no fear of any other critters. I think mice in animated movies are cute and I delight in their antics, but until mice resemble Mickey or Minnie, they are not welcome at our house.

Deceleration of Time

I am about to inquire about my chances of joining The Society for the Deceleration of Time. Hopefully there is a branch nearby.

It seems I am constantly in overdrive. Now, the approaching Christmas season revs me into super overdrive. Even with that surge of power, why does it seem that there are not enough hours in the day? I know I am not the only one being challenged.

A friend of mine (frantically trying to get his choir ready for a Christmas musical) said: "Three more days added to each of the weeks in December would help!"

Don't get me wrong. In spite of its rash commercialism, I love the Christmas season. I love the warm glow of the lights in the unique arrangements of outdoor decorations in our neighbourhood. I love decorated trees and family gatherings. I love the shopping for gifts for loved ones and the inner satisfaction I feel from the giving of money and food to the needy. I love the season's special foods like Christmas cake, plum pudding, shortbread cookies, and gingerbread houses. I love the "Away in a Manger" sacred music and the Santa Claus secular music that carols through the malls and echoes from radio and TV. I love the sending and receiving of Christmas cards. I love the Christmas concerts at schools and churches. I love the once-a-year Christmas TV specials.

I may be approaching my seventh decade, but I still reserve time to watch such children's movies as *The Grinch Who Stole Christmas* or *Rudolph the Red-Nosed Reindeer*, ever thankful to my grandchildren who introduced these to me many years ago. With daily newscasts reminding us of the unhappiness caused by greed, wars, and general apathy, I more than ever need the simplicity of hearing how Christmas came to Whoville in spite of such problems. I need to see the Grinch's heart grow. I need to be reminded through the story of Rudolph that even seeming misfits can change hopeless situations. Love makes it all possible.

So why am I in super overdrive? It's because all these good things are crammed into one month, and sometimes, if we are late-starters, they are jam-packed into the last couple of weeks.

Optimistically, as an old song suggests, we could celebrate the spirit of Christmas all year long. I wonder how many of us it would take to bravely step outside the box so that it would become commonplace to say "Seasons' Greetings" and to show love and the spirit of giving all year.

I do know two families who for various reasons have their Christmas family meal in September. The families are large and the adult children and their families are scattered across the Province. At their fall gathering, gifts are exchanged, there is time for visiting, and they enjoy a catered meal. Their December is far less hectic than mine.

I think The Society for the Deceleration of Time must be a very slow-growing group (How apropos!) because it has acquired only eight hundred members since its 1990 conception in Austria. If enough of us gradually embrace the concept of the "deceleration of time" in our own family, the ripple we start might keep spreading. It's just possible that the spirit of Christmas, that caring for others, could be extended for several months.

Change is one of the most difficult things in life. Nonetheless, I feel a talk with my family coming on!

"Dinosaur" Penmanship

I'm sure that many of my former grade five pupils remember me as the teacher who required that they "earn" their pens. Yes, one of the big attractions in grade five was that pupils were given pens, ballpoints to be sure, but nonetheless, a pen. In those years (early 1990s), handwriting lessons were still part of the curriculum. Each day we had a time set aside — especially in grades three and four — in which pupils practised cursive writing. Sometimes it would be just one letter that they would write over and over, trying to match the model I had outlined on the board. Then, we would choose a word that had that letter in it. So it might have been that the letter "b" was repeated line by line, and then the word "baby".

Writing in pencil is very forgiving; mistakes can be erased. Writing in ink is a whole different story. I frowned on an ugly slash crossing out mistakes. I preferred brackets. Because I had been an elementary student in the age of daily penmanship drills in which we made uniform circles, lines of slanted vertical strokes, all with a fountain pen, I took great pride in my penmanship skills. Now, as a teacher, I expected the same from my students, but I wanted to make it fun. I had math games, spelling games, phys ed games, why not penmanship games?

Thus began the challenge for each student to earn his/her "pen licence". I created a certificate that was presented, along with the pen, to each deserving student. Most parents applauded this procedure and took as much joy in the licensing as their child did. By the end of the year, each student was writing with pen in neat and legible handwriting.

I retired in 1995, and, by then, I doubt if there were any Ontario schools that did not have a bank of computers. Now every classroom has a computer and every house usually has more than one. I am writing this in the year 2009, the year of blogging, the Blackberry, Facebook and Twittering. Who concerns themselves with handwriting in the younger generation?

Coupled with the demise of good penmanship is friendly -letter writing. Text-messages are preferred. With some young people, webcams are used instead of telephones. I suppose it's of some benefit to see the person to whom you are talking. It would certainly not be the thing for me who likes to talk on the phone while I relax in my pj's.

I once thought that I would like to explore the possibility of analyzing handwriting to reveal personality traits. It was exciting to know that crime solvers hire trained people to do this. How valid is it now, I wonder.

When I receive a card from an older person, I still admire their fine handwriting but I know it's a dying art. From the straight pen that required constant dipping of its nib in a bottle of ink to the fountain pen (first having an inner tube, then later cartridges of ink) to the ballpoint, we of a certain age have been schooled in cursive writing. Many of us remember applying blotting paper to each line we wrote so the ink did not smear.

Recently, I attended the fiftieth wedding anniversary of a couple in their seventies. The guests enjoyed leafing through the wedding book that had been penned at wedding time by the bride. All the attendants' names were recorded as well as the important details of the ceremony. So many of those looking at the book commented on the bride's beautiful handwriting, and this led to discussions about present-day grandchildren and how their handwriting is illegible. Several in the group remarked that many of their older grandchildren resort to printing when they have to record anything that cannot be done on the computer.

Personally? I do appreciate the computer. It's my right hand. However, I still take great pride in my penmanship.

Should I apologize to all those students who laboured to earn a pen? If any of you felt tortured, I'm sorry. To those who thought it was fun, God bless you! I would like to think, that on occasion, you still take pride in your handwriting. We still have to sign our names to make things legal.

As for those of you who became doctors, I know there are exceptions to every rule! I'll just have to have faith when you write out my prescription.

Electronic Pastimes vs. Traditional

Will on-line books replace the good old-fashioned books? That has been the question for several years now. If the line-up at the bookstores at Christmas time is any indication, the answer is no.

Personally, I need to hold the book in my hands to really enjoy it. I want to be comfy as I read, to be able to turn to a previous page. I could never treasure an on-line print-out the way I treasure my books.

The same is true of our cottage pastimes. Frank and I are "plugged-in" there, able to access the Internet (albeit by dial-up) and e-mail while we holiday. I am happy to be classed as computer-savvy, but I doubt if I could ever be content to make this my sole tool of communication. I'm happy to receive friendly e-mails, but I'm even happier to answer the telephone and hear a friend's voice.

Although Frank plays solitaire and chess on-line, he still looks forward to our evening game of cribbage and loves a good game of euchre when there are more than the two of us.

Facing your human partner, dealing the cards, chatting. How much better this is than the coldness of the computer screen.

This week as we take a winter break at our cottage, we are enjoying the challenge of a jigsaw puzzle. Setting up a new puzzle over the Christmas holiday is a tradition with us. This one is a real test, but I feel confident we'll finish it and it will join the others that adorn our cottage walls. This morning, as we were fitting pieces into the puzzle, we laughed about how an analysis of the jigsaw process might lead to us being labelled "weird", maybe even "crazy". A perfectly beautiful picture had been chopped up on purpose into intricate, small pieces that we are now concentrating on as to how to reconstruct. In defence, I might argue that we are exercising our brains. I have read that puzzle-solving is one thing recommended to help prevent Alzheimer's disease. If so, it's a definite bonus for us who enjoy the simple challenge of a puzzle.

In our church community, a yearly intergenerational crokinole party is held. I'm thinking it should be monthly. It would be difficult to find anything to match the laughing, the happy shrieks of joy, and the camaraderie shared as we wrestle with the task of shooting those "cookies" toward where we hope they will go.

My grandchildren never go anywhere — even to the next room, it seems — without their iPods (or the latest technological device), yet their enthusiasm for this old-fashioned game is refreshing. When the crokinole party idea was introduced five or six years ago, few of our youth knew the word, or the game. How quickly it became a hit! Blackberrys and iPods are left at home.

Intergenerational fun at the
crokinole party!

There are some hobbies the computer can never replace. Knitting, crocheting, woodworking, artistic painting, and golfing are only a few.

Some hobbies and skills have been enhanced by electronics. The world of photography and photo-developing is one, writing is another.

As a musician, I am thrilled to be able to choose music on-line, hear it on-line, and place my order for books or CD's through on-line sites. Still, nothing on-line quite compares with getting together in person with an instrumental group to play music, or to join a group to sing.

I hope there will always be enough gregarious, community-minded people to organize activities in which we interact with one another. Sitting alone, facing only my computer screen, will never be enough for me. Facebook is a great "tool" that enhances life and provides another "face" but it lacks the comforting touch. I still want the "warm fuzzy" feeling of personal contact.

Now, back to facing Frank and the conversations that will ensue as we complete that puzzle!

Income Tax Madness

I hate even the *thought* of getting my papers together at income tax time. I procrastinate as long as I can. Everything about it irritates me.

Like most people, I grumble about the amount of money the government strips from me all year long, but my main grudge is about the amount of time it takes to assemble the papers — and the time spent at the accountant's.

I have tried at times to set up a filing system so that when April rolls around, the needed receipts, statements, and documents are easier to find. Being a bit of a miser, I recycle file folders. I'm an organist so have a surplus of files that once held choir music. The titles of anthems are still on the edges of folders.

Even in my state of frustration, I laughed when I realized that, purely by coincidence, my household expenses were in a folder labelled "Come with Your Heartache". Likewise, my writing expenses were filed in "I Just Keep Trusting My Lord".

When all the sweating, the muttering, the adding and the subtracting are done and I'm ultimately finished at the accountant's this year — probably just before the tax department's deadline — I am hoping I won't have cause to file the final results in the folder labelled "I Surrender All".

"Another Time, Another Place"

Close your eyes and picture yourself on a horse-drawn, wooden-plank sleigh covered up with a heavy buffalo robe (yes, real buffalo hide) on a frosty winter morning. Jack and Fred, the two strong, honey-coloured Clydesdales, exhale great streams of hoary crystals from their nostrils as they work in even rhythm, heedless of their passengers nestled behind. The world is quiet except for the steady *clip-clopping* of their hooves. They know the trail; they have pulled this sleigh to the woodlot many times already this winter.

That scene is still vivid in the mind of my husband, Frank, who was raised on an Ontario farm in Lake St. Peter, North Hastings County. For at least ten of those boyhood years in the forties and fifties, he was his father's helper in cutting hardwood trees for family firewood or for logs to sell.

Frank's father, Buster (no one ever called him by his real name, Wilfred), stoked the wood stove in the kitchen each winter morning to rid their rustic farmhouse of its bone-chilling cold. Twice a week, after a breakfast of bacon, eggs, and toast, it was time to hitch up the horses and spend the day at the woodlot. One of the trip's essentials never left behind was the lunch that was packed by Winnie, Frank's mother.

Most farms had a summer kitchen. It was a ritual to use this for summer cooking but as soon as the cold weather arrived, farm meals were again centred in the regular kitchen. The un-heated summer kitchen would then be used only for storage.

Frank remembers the pig carcasses that hung frozen in their summer kitchen. As pork was needed, a slab would be cut off and roasted. This provided the wonderful filling for the sand-wiches. The generous slices of roasted pork would be tucked between thick slices of homemade bread that Winnie had baked the day before in the cook-stove oven. She wrapped these sand-wiches in waxed paper, carefully packing them in an old army-surplus haversack.

Later, as stomach growling and the sun overhead indi-cated lunchtime was approaching, Frank and his father headed to the clearing where they built their fires. Buster wasted no time retrieving two tin sauce dishes and two Crown corn syrup pails that he had left in the designated spot beside a stump. One pail was full of frozen syrup, the other held a package of tea — loose-leaf tea. Setting the package aside, Buster filled that pail with snow and set it over the fire to make water for the tea. (Frank reminds me that they avoided any yellow snow!) The other pail was put over the fire so the frozen contents would thaw into warm, delicious, syrup. With that duty done, they opened the haversack to pull out the pork sandwiches, now frozen solid. These were masterfully hoisted over the fire on two wooden sticks fashioned for that purpose.

Frank has yet to find anything that tasted quite as good as this lunch of toasted pork sandwiches accompanied by sauce dishes of warm, golden corn syrup. The aroma of their roasted pork added to the fragrance of the spruce and balsam trees that surrounded them. The carpet of pristine snow sparkled in the sunlight; chickadees and blue jays provided the background music.

Changes in life are inevitable. Memories are a blessing.